TRIAL
AND
TRIBULATION

A WILD HERITANCE TALE

COMPANION STORY TO *TRIAL RUN*

S. LYNN HELTON

Trial and Tribulation is a work of fiction.
Names, characters, places, organizations, and events are either
products of the author's imagination or are used fictitiously. Any
resemblance to actual persons, living or dead, organizations,
events, or locales is entirely coincidental.

ISBN (Paperback): 978-1-7348581-0-5
ISBN (eBook): 978-1-7348581-1-2

Scripturio Books
www.ScripturioBooks.com
24.04.08

DEDICATION

For Mark, who wanted to hear Aahmes' side.

ACKNOWLEDGMENTS

With many thanks to my beta-readers, who greatly helped improve the story, and to my family, who so patiently answered the odd story questions I put to them.

A NOTE ABOUT THE STORY'S TIMELINE

If you've read *Trial Run*, you'll find a few events in *Trial and Tribulation* familiar. That's because the two stories are very intertwined, their timelines overlapping.

CHAPTER 1

The one sound Aahmes most dreaded to hear at a time like this drifted through the otherwise silent house: the sound of someone else's voice.

"My sweeting?" a woman's voice called out from somewhere in the gloom. "I left the gathering early, as your note asked."

Aahmes froze then cursed to himself. He had not expected Lord Walrard's lover to be in the house this night. After some thought, he remembered her name: Lady Hadelin. Both she and Walrard were supposed to be at gatherings with other nobles. Such things usually ran until well past dawn, a time still at least a candle-mark away.

Maybe he should abandon this before he was discovered. He could just come back….

No, he couldn't.

Within a day, Lord Walrard was departing Rhadanthus – probably the most decrepit city in the Six Realms of the Monarch. Word had it that the noble did not intend to return. So this was Aahmes' one chance at the riches secreted in the man's house.

He grinned. Avoiding the noble's lover might be both entertaining and a challenge. He would just see what he could get away with.

He eased the door closed behind him and looked around the room. The kitchen, as he had expected. There should be servants' stairs nearby to take him to the floor above. He hoped Hadelin did not wake any servants.

He found the stairs he wanted tucked in a corner near more stairs that headed down, probably to a food cellar. Maybe he would grab some tasty tidbit on his way out.

Lady Hadelin did not speak again. She had probably figured out that Lord Walrard was not there. Would she stay, wait for his return? Or go back out?

One foot on the servants' stairs, Aahmes lingered and listened. A sound of soft footsteps came from the hallway beyond the kitchen. Just his luck. Hadelin must have decided she needed something to eat or drink.

He scurried up the stairs, keeping his steps light, nearly soundless. He paused in the shadows at the top of the stairs to watch and listen again.

No one had shuttered the windows in the kitchen, so while the stairs were shadowed, enough light from the risen moons shone in the room below to let him see Hadelin's fancy silk skirt brush by the bottom of the staircase.

She muttered something about pastries. Aahmes shook his head in disgust. One would think she would have gotten enough to eat already at whichever noble's gathering she had attended.

He hesitated as that thought led to another. She would be wearing jewelry. A lot, if glimpses he had caught of her before this night were any indication.

But to get it, he would have to tie her somewhere and make sure she never saw his face. Too many complications. Better to make sure she never saw him at all.

After her skirt moved out of sight, he turned to the passage at his back and studied it.

A small door to his left opened to another narrow staircase going up. To the servants' rooms at the top of the house, no doubt.

In the passage he faced, one wall held narrow windows made of many small panes of glass held together in lattices of wood. Half of the windows were shuttered. Doors ran along the opposite wall. From what he had been able to learn, Lord Walrard's suite was at the end of the hall, until recently shared with his wife who had since left him. If Walrard followed the pattern of most nobles in the city, many of his riches would be there.

Aahmes smiled when he noticed the rug that ran the length of the hall. That would help muffle his footsteps.

Swift and silent, he headed to the last doors, double doors that looked black in the dim light. The rug under his feet was worn in spots. Odd.

One of the double doors stood ajar. He paused to listen then eased that door open further and slipped inside. He left the door the way he had found it and looked around.

Aahmes found himself in a small room, sparsely furnished. A door in the wall across from him stood open, letting in minimal light from the window in that room. Some light also followed him into the room from the door ajar behind him.

After his eyes adjusted to the light in this room, dimmer than that in the hall, he glided to the door opposite and checked that room. The bedroom, as he had anticipated, unoccupied and with a neglected feel to it.

He turned back to the outer room. A few steps took him to the single desk and chair in the room. The rug on the floor here, too, was more worn than he would have expected.

The desk was plain, not much more than a table with three drawers. A look through the drawers revealed nothing worthwhile, only several letters from various merchants and other nobles. He carried a few to the better light in the doorway to the bedroom. Every letter he skimmed made mention of Lord Walrard owing the person the letter was from.

With a grimace, Aahmes stared at the papers he held. He might have wasted his time coming here.

He gave himself a slight shake and returned the letters to the desk. Nothing else in the room looked promising so he moved to the bedroom.

Again, sparse furnishings and signs of wear characterized this room. Bedding that had seen better days lay piled on the bed. A quick, but thorough search through it and under the mattress produced nothing but lint and gritty dust. The mattress itself smelled old and Aahmes found no hint of anything hidden within it.

The chest at the foot of the bed held clothing and nothing else.

Moving faster, feeling that his time was running out, Aahmes next turned to the single wardrobe, much plainer than usual for a noble. Few clothes hung within, and they, too, looked worn. But on the floor of the wardrobe, he found a wooden box, tucked back in the corner. A coffer, he hoped.

When he tried to lift it out, he discovered that it was secured to the floor somehow. And the lid would not lift.

Must be locked.

He pulled his lockpicks from one of his belt pouches and soon had the box unlocked. While he tucked the lockpicks away again, he heard a sound he dreaded almost as much as a voice in a supposedly empty house.

Close behind him came a huffing, puffing sound, which changed to a low growl as Aahmes slowly turned. When his gaze met that of the small fur-puff that stood no taller than his shins, the creature began to bark.

Aahmes cursed. How could he have forgotten about Hadelin's little yappy lapdog?

He flipped open the box in the wardrobe and grabbed the contents. At the same time, he heard Hadelin calling out.

His time had run out.

The annoying lapdog nipped at his ankles and continued raising a fuss, even darting between his feet and nearly tripping him. He stumbled and swayed to avoid kicking or stepping on the noisy fur-puff as he scrambled to the window.

Cringing at the hurried footsteps that approached, he flipped the latch and yanked the window open. One of the small panes of glass that made up the window fell out with his motion and shattered on the floor at his feet. He winced at the crash and hauled himself through the narrow window to hang from his hands, shortening the drop to the ground below. The irritating fur-puff jumped up and nipped one of his fingers before he could let go.

Leafless bushes helped break his fall, and at the same time snagged his cloak and tore a strip from it. Cursing, he snatched the piece of cloth and ran, disappearing into the night, his gray cloak helping him blend into the shadows.

He heard Lady Hadelin shouting for the City Warders as he rounded a corner. He paused to brush broken twigs from his clothes so they would not drop and leave a trail, then he hurried away.

~ ~ ~

Stunning, and at the same time disappointing. That was the only way to describe them.

Crouched in a tight alcove in a narrow alley, Aahmes glowered at the handful of small gems he held. He stirred them with a finger but, of course, that did nothing to increase their value. These were not worth anything close to what he had planned to come away with that night. He suspected a few of them were false, too.

But how was he to have known that Lord Walrard was

almost destitute, his fine house not much more than a stripped shell of its former glory? Every indication had been that the man had no shortage of wealth.

That's what comes of rushing a job, he told himself. But when word is that the quarry plans to leave the city soon, likely for good, what choice does a guy have?

Still he scowled at the gems. A nice enough haul for an average Shadower, he mused. But he was not the average Shadower. He was one of the best of that guild of thieves and sellswords. He relished that distinction, had worked hard to achieve it, and he needed to make sure it stayed that way.

Aahmes wrapped his cloak tighter around himself against the winter-end chill in the air. Too late to grab anything else for the night. He had spent far too much time at a tavern before he visited that noble's house. Sure, he could pilfer something more from some of the houses that did not get busy too early in the day….

His stomach growled, putting an end to that thought. He raked his chin-length shaggy black hair back from his face and worked to convince himself that just this once bringing back a small haul would not ruin his hard-won standing as best in the guild.

He tucked the gems back in their velvet pouch and tucked that into his shirt under his layered tunics, next to his skin above his belt. Better steal some breakfast, that way he would not diminish his haul for the night. The city's open-air markets should be open soon. One was not too far from Shadow Keep, the Shadowers' whimsically named dilapidated home. Along with something to eat, maybe he'd pick up some coins or worthwhile goods to bring back with him.

He glanced at the thin sliver of sky visible between the buildings, tinged with the light of the coming dawn. He would probably get to the market before it opened for the day. Still, moving would help keep him warm.

He unfolded himself from his tight alcove and headed

toward the ring of the city where he would find that market. Out of habit, Aahmes used back streets and alleys for most of the way there. Even if he was far from the noble's house, he had no desire to draw any attention from the Warders if he could help it. Best to stay unseen.

The streets and alleys were more empty than busy, but he saw signs of the city beginning to wake. Before long, more people walked the streets as they started the day's business. Aahmes yawned. He decided to forgo trying to add to the night's haul this once and just get a bit to eat then head back to the Keep for some overdue sleep.

A few streets away from the market, a sensation of being watched crawled across his back and arms. So he already half-expected the scraping sound that came from behind him.

This alley was seldom used except by folks like him. He had a sudden feeling he knew what he would see when he turned around. He stopped and turned, unsurprised to find himself facing two of the city's rascals.

Both older than Aahmes, the two dressed much like him in shirts, layered tunics, and trousers. Theirs were little better than rags, where Aahmes' were just very worn. The man taller and bulkier than both his companion and Aahmes, with skin much lighter than Aahmes' own skin, had unkempt brown hair that hung in his eyes. He clenched and unclenched his large fists, grinning all the while.

The other man stood of a height with Aahmes, his hair as black as Aahmes', although much shorter and tightly curled, and his skin darker than Aahmes'. He scrutinized Aahmes, his expression deliberate and thoughtful.

"What a nice surprise, meetin' yeh out an' about in th' city this fine mornin', Aahms m' friend," the skinnier man greeted him with a self-satisfied smile.

"It's Aahmes, Berz."

"Oh, sure, sure." Both men stepped closer to Aahmes. "I just been tellin' Gwel here how much I missed yeh.

Missed yeh mixin' with us, with the rout." He planted his fists on his hips and stared down Aahmes' skeptical look at the word. When Aahmes had run with these two, and some others, only one of the bands of thieving rascals in the city had called themselves a rout, an old name for a band of people.

"Yah, we're a reg'lar rout now," Berz declared. "Such lively times we used t' have. But now them so-lofty Shadowers've got their fists on yeh. Yeh need t' come back with us."

Aahmes heard the unmistakable sound of a footstep behind him. That made three of them. Not good.

He shrugged, with a lazy grin for Berz. "Why would I want to mix with you anymore? I'm good where I'm at now. And I met the deal long back to go my own way. The rout has no claim on me."

"Yeh cheated," Berz snarled. "Somehow. Yeh must've. No one could've met th' deal so fast elsewise."

With a scornful look, Aahmes shook his head. "None of you, that's for certain."

"Hah! I say yeh still owe us. As leader's second now, I say yeh need t' come back with us."

"Amazing that the rout can run at all with you as leader's second."

Berz and Gwel exchanged glances. "Get him!" Berz shouted and they both lunged for Aahmes.

But Aahmes had expected the move. After partnering in the past with this small band for several seasons, he knew how they worked.

He dodged both men's attacks and shoved Berz in the back as he stumbled past, sending him into the third person, Phrae, another he remembered from his time with them. A deceptively delicate-looking woman with pale-yellow hair and beige skin, she might be the most dangerous of the three rascals.

Aahmes drew his daggers, prepared to show them how far removed he was from his time with them when his sour luck of the night continued. Two Warders rounded the corner at the end of the alley and shouted at them when they spotted the fight.

Ignoring the others, and the Warders, Aahmes sheathed his daggers and leapt for the wall to his right. He scrambled up its rough surface to the roof and ran, jumping several narrow alleys. He knew those three would not follow: Gwelasius would not be able to climb that wall, Phrae did not like heights, and nothing would get Berz to face him without the others.

Aahmes smiled at the ruckus behind him in the alley. Those three never seemed to learn that sometimes it was better to run, especially when the Warders came. Aahmes had not yet been caught by a Warder and he had no intention of that changing.

Several streets away, a loose shingle turned under Aahmes' foot when he landed on it and he fell, slipping back toward the gap he had just jumped. He grasped at the roof beneath him, splinters slicing into his hands, and dug in with the toes of his boots, managing to stop his slide right at the edge of the roof. At a shout from below, he peered over the edge, nearly losing his grip. A boy stood at the end of the alley below, pointing at him and shouting for the Warders. That was enough to urge him up and away again.

When he felt certain no one pursued him, he found a hidden spot on the current rooftop to huddle and catch his breath. From there, he would need to drop back down to the streets, and he did not want to show that he had just been running. That would raise questions, even in this part of the city.

While he rested, he picked the splinters of wood out of his hands – more smarting annoyances to add to the lingering sting from the lapdog's bite. At least his ankle did not hurt much, only an ache really. Nothing much he could do about it yet, although he did tear a long strip from his cloak to wrap it.

After his breathing slowed to normal, he put his boot back on then eased himself over the side of the roof and back to the ground in yet another narrow alley. He brushed himself off and pulled up the hood of his cloak. The air was still cold enough, despite the bright sunshine, that wearing his hood would not look unusual.

His path across the rooftops had taken him at an angle away from the market he wanted so he trudged back that direction.

Close to a half candle-mark later, Aahmes reached the market. By then, most of the merchants had already set out their wares and many perspective buyers walked the curved road.

Aahmes joined the press of people, matching his pace to theirs while he looked for something to eat.

Without thinking about it, he also kept some of his attention on the crowd. And so he saw the girl with dark brown skin and long twists of brown hair swipe something from one merchant's table while the woman spoke with her neighbor.

He knew that girl: Zwena, a learner with only a couple of seasons with the Shadowers, so far. If she was there, then her partner Orran—another new, young apprentice— would be, too. And that meant this ring's market street must be the one *that* tyro Namid had chosen to fulfill her assignment today.

Aahmes frowned, with a sigh. Four of them at one market would be too many, even if only one of them was a true Shadower. Trying to ignore the complaints from his empty stomach, he took himself into a side alley and climbed again to the rooftops. Might as well see how the apprentices accomplished their task.

~ ~ ~

From a perch on the roof of a nearby tavern, Aahmes watched the three apprentice Shadowers and saw the two younger ones botch further thievery attempts. He doubted their task that morning had them trying their hands at such thievery yet, anyway. He observed Namid, the more experienced of the three, salvage the job they had all been assigned, in effect doing all their assignments herself through a combination of skill and a bit of luck.

Too bad she had managed to pull off her task, in spite of her inept helpers. That put her that much closer to becoming a full Shadower; something he would rather not see. He enjoyed his reputation in the guild for his skill. Yet this slip of a girl—who had appeared out of nowhere—already rivaled his abilities.

And worse, the other Shadowers seemed to delight in teasing him about how much they resembled each other – with their similar features, red-brown skin and straight, dark hair. Bad enough that she threatened to match him, maybe even surpass him, but she *would* have to look like she could be his younger sister, too.

When he realized most of his attention had rested on her, he shook his head at himself and brushed his hair back from his face with one hand.

Why did she have to be so good?

CHAPTER 2

Back in Shadow Keep, Aahmes grabbed a few scraps of food left in the kitchen from the morning meal and headed to the third floor to his room, shared with another Shadower. Pleased to see the other man was not there, he gulped the food to quiet his stomach's complaints then fell onto his narrow bed, asleep before too long.

He woke a few candle-marks later, hungry again. But first, he needed to hand over the little he had managed to collect the previous night. He should have done that when he first returned to the Keep.

He shrugged off his cloak—which he had slept in—and tossed it on his bed. The missing corner piece was not nearly as obvious as it had been, since he had torn that strip to bind his ankle. Maybe he would just leave the cloak with a ragged bottom, rather than make any repairs. He pulled out the piece the bushes had torn and dropped it next to his cloak, then stepped out into the hallway, pleased to note that his ankle only twinged a little.

Turning to his right, he took the stairs down to the second floor and headed to the small room next to the room the Shadowers' leader Dar liked to call his office.

The person who was supposed to collect what everyone had gathered the previous night might still be there sorting through everything.

Passing Dar's closed door, Aahmes heard voices. He paused to listen and recognized Namid's voice.

"And that's it," she said. "The whole mess."

Aahmes heard Dar's voice then. "I'll have words with them. But I see no reason their actions will affect your status here. You recovered well and finished your task. You're ready to face your Trial."

Aahmes scowled and moved off, having heard enough. If she passed her Trial, a test of her thievery and weapons skills, she would be considered a full member of the Shadowers.

The next door stood open and he entered. The room's occupant looked up from her task at the table and frowned.

Aahmes frowned right back at her. The beige-skinned, brown-haired woman, Aerill, normally worked as one of the Shadowers' weapons instructors. Must be her turn today to fill in for Dar's Second, Thes, who most often handled this task.

"What've you got for me, oh great thief who's unable to bring his collection by first thing like everyone else?" Aerill demanded.

Aahmes pulled out the small pouch of gems and dropped it with a flourish on the table in front of her. "Something no doubt better than all this other…stuff everyone else brought in."

"We'll see about that," she muttered as she pulled open the drawstrings on the pouch.

While she poured the contents into one hand, Aahmes took a seat in the other chair in the room and stretched his legs out, lounging indolently. "I suspect some of them are false," he told her.

Aerill rolled the gems in her hand back and forth. "I think you're right. But only a couple, I'd say. This is far less than your usual. Might be you're losing your touch." She peered at him.

Aahmes winced to himself but let none of his concern show on his face. "Anyone can have an off night," he said. "Doesn't mean anything." He waved a hand at the meager collection of items on her table and the shelves around the room. "Still better than anyone else managed last night, from the looks of it."

She acknowledged the truth of that, although she looked none too happy to do so. She plucked one small gem from the bunch and held it out to Aahmes. "Your portion, for now," she told him. "And I know that one's real. Come back later after I've gone through the rest to see if you get any more from last night's haul."

Aahmes gave her a smug grin and took the gem. "Of course."

As he walked away, he smiled to himself. Even when he had a bad night, he was still unmatched.

When he passed Dar's door, the Shadowers' leader called out to him. "Aahmes, a word."

Aahmes joined the older man in his office and closed the door at Dar's gesture. Not that it would keep anything they said very private, as Aahmes knew.

With a questioning look for Dar, he grabbed a chair and perched on it.

Dar began to pace, his light brown skin with its smattering of freckles florid with his agitation. "You've seen our take from last night?"

Aahmes nodded. Where was this going?

Dar rubbed a hand across his disheveled auburn hair then along his jaw, cleanshaven as Aahmes' was also. "Several of the newer Shadowers have reported more, and more hurtful, run-ins with some of those roaming groups of rascals. Specifically that one you used to mix with before you came to us."

Aahmes grimaced. "They're calling themselves a rout now. But they can't possibly think they can take us on."

Dar shrugged. "Have they tried to get you to go back with them?"

Apprehension crawled through Aahmes. "Not exactly," he said, stretching his words out. "Three of them waylaid me this morning. One *did* say something about mixing with them again." He gazed at Dar, his expression tense. "I didn't think anything of it."

Dar sat in the chair behind his table and studied Aahmes with a thoughtful expression.

"Would you go mix with them again?"

Aahmes started. "No! I'm a Shadower." His apprehension deepened. Was he going to have to leave to protect them?

"Could they come to believe you'd consider going back? If so, you might learn what's behind these actions of theirs."

Aahmes frowned and shook his head. "I don't know. We're not friendly, not even really on speaking terms."

After some thought, Dar stood again. "Well, think on it. It could be helpful to us. And there's no one else who can pull it off."

Aahmes winced. He knew what Dar was doing, appealing to his pride. But that did not make him wrong.

"I *will* think on it and let you know," he said as he left.

Aahmes grabbed some bread and cheese from the Keep's kitchen to make a midday meal and took it outside. He stood in the sun while he ate and pondered what the rout might be plotting.

He had not come to any conclusions when he finished his meal, except he had decided that he *would* look into it as Dar had indirectly asked, *maybe* even pretend that he was considering mixing again with the rout, if it looked like that would help.

After he told Dar his decision, he headed to the common hall—the large room on the main floor where everyone liked to gather—still distracted by thoughts of the rout and his memories of his time with them. Small-time thieves and thugs as they were, they should not be going after a group as large and well-organized as the Shadowers. They should not be able to.

He paused inside the doorway and looked around. Most of the people there sat at the scarred tables, drinks at hand, dicing. Even that tyro was carrying a cup to a table where Jaikrein—an older woman with pale skin, eyes and hair—greeted her and held out some dice.

Aahmes wandered over to their table in time to hear Jaikrein tease Namid about having beginner's luck. Remembering how Namid had managed to salvage her task earlier in the market, in spite of the fiasco it had become, Aahmes agreed with the older Shadower.

"She seems to be filled with it," he added, taking a seat at the table. He met Namid's scowl with a neutral gaze of his own as his thoughts drifted back to the tangle that was the rout problem. What could they be thinking?

The two women continued their dice game. Jaikrein even offered to let him join, although a glare accompanied the offer. Not too surprising. Aahmes already knew she did not like him much. He returned her gaze, his own expression aloof, and shook his head. He had no interest in dice right then.

To distract himself from thoughts of the rout, he studied Namid. Interesting that she seemed to have held the knowledge of her readiness for her Trial to herself. Most would have shouted it to all their friends in the guild already. She returned his gaze, her own seemed tinged with apprehension.

"Word is that you're ready for your Trial," Aahmes said, watching to see how she would react.

He noted her start of surprise, quickly hidden.

"So soon?" Jaikrein said, with a big, gap-toothed grin for Namid.

Namid pointedly turned away from Aahmes to remind Jaikrein that she had already been an apprentice Shadower for two years. Aahmes had the feeling Namid was trying to irritate him by ignoring him. Didn't bother him.

Their talk turned to who would design Namid's Trial and Aahmes spoke up without thinking.

"I offer my services." His wicked grin conveyed the challenge he was issuing to Namid.

Namid peered at Aahmes with narrowed eyes.

What was she thinking? If it was anything like 'what is he *thinking*?' then it matched his own thoughts. What *had* he been thinking to offer to design her Trial? He did not want to have anything to do with it. Although it occurred to him, as her eyes narrowed further, that it might be a way to get her out of the guild. If he could arrange it right.

When Jaikrein warned Namid against having Aahmes design her Trial, he gave the older Shadower a withering look.

"I wouldn't come up with a Trial that was unavoidably fatal. But the Trial *is* supposed to test tyros' abilities, to see if they can hold their own and belong with us. If she can't handle it, it'll be clear to everyone that she doesn't belong here with the Shadowers." Aahmes shrugged to indicate how he felt about that, his action deliberately nonchalant.

"So *generous* of you to offer to help a lowly tyro such as me," Namid said to Aahmes, her voice and smile both overly sweet. "I think having you design my Trial is an absolutely *wonderful* idea. Then when I pass, there'll be no question that I'm good enough. It'll be clear to *everyone*, as you said."

Aahmes gave her a sharp look, somewhat surprised that she would actually accept his offer. Then he recognized the counterchallenge she offered via her expression. He managed a thin smile for her.

They settled on a couple days from then to start her Trial. When Namid claimed she would be ready, Aahmes scoffed.

He sauntered away then to go see Dar and let him know about the Trial arrangements, already wondering how he was going to do this, devise something challenging enough to get her out of the guild. He had never before designed a Trial.

In passing, he exchanged a few casual greetings with some friends, but his mind was elsewhere. Now he had two problems: this cursed Trial that he had gotten himself involved in, and the mess with the rout.

With a grimace for this madness, he trudged up the stairs, headed back to Dar's office.

CHAPTER 3

As he approached the door to Dar's office, Aahmes' steps slowed. What had he just done to himself?

He paused out of sight of the opening. Why take on her Trial design? He did not want to *help* her become a full member of the guild.

"I can tell you're out there. Might as well come on in," Dar said from within his office.

Aahmes eased around the doorway and into the room. And he stood there, uncertain what to say.

Dar looked up from whatever he was working on, a ring and some papers. "Aahmes? Hadn't expected to see you again so soon. Have you already got something for me?"

Aahmes sighed and shook his head. "Not yet. I'll see what I can learn this afternoon. I've, uh…just now promised something…."

Dar scrutinized the younger man. "What've you done?"

Aahmes raked his hand through his hair and looked away from Dar's gaze. "Said I'd design Namid's Trial."

"What?" Dar exploded, causing Aahmes to flinch. "What are you playing at?"

"Nothing! I just blurted it out when she and Jaikrein were talking about who might design her Trial."

"Well, you can just go tell her you made a mistake and you won't be able to do it."

Aahmes turned to go, then stopped himself.

"No," he said, drawing the word out. "I don't think I can. Jaikrein heard me say I'd do it. I can't back out."

Dar threw his hands up in the air. "You can't back out? Aahmes, you've not designed a Trial before. You're not that far removed from when you passed your own. Your precious reputation won't suffer if you don't do this."

Aahmes glared at the older man. "So you're ordering me to back out?"

Dar met his sullen look then sighed and sank back into his chair.

"No, I'm not ordering you to." He rubbed his forehead as if his head pained him. "You two with your rivalry. I *will* order you to strictly follow the rules we have for designing Trials."

Aahmes tried to ease the tension that had built in him at Dar's disapproval. He worked to make his voice sound reasonable. "And what are those?"

Dar caught his gaze with his own. "First, challenging. Neither the thievery nor the weapons portion can be too easy. But then I know that won't be an issue with you two. But neither can they be too dangerous. We're not trying to kill off any potential members who show they aren't capable."

Aahmes nodded and fought his grin. He had no intention of making anything easy for that tyro.

Dar continued. "Next, you're allowed during the Trial to create no more than three difficulties, smaller challenges if you will, that apprentices can expect to encounter as one of us, out on one of our tasks. Difficulties that aren't a true part of the Trial's main task. And you don't inform the apprentice of these ahead of time."

"I'd not heard of that part." With a sharp look for Dar,

he thought back to his own Trial. "That explains a few things I remember wondering about."

"Keep these lesser challenges truly lesser," Dar said.

Aahmes nodded again but his thoughts had latched onto a possible theft that would well-nigh ensure that Namid failed to gain final acceptance into the Shadowers. He let the idea roll around in his mind and so paid little attention when Dar said that the theft must also be something that the designer was capable of, without help.

When Dar stopped talking, Aahmes gave him a quizzical look. "That's it?"

Dar's expression turned hard. "That's it. And I'll allow this *only* if Namid tells me herself that she agrees to it. And nothing underhanded for the Trial. Understood?"

Aahmes nodded his agreement. "Understood." With the idea he had, he would not need anything underhanded.

"When will you be ready to present your Trial idea?" Dar said.

"Present it?"

"Yes. Remember how it was for your own Trial? As the Trial overseer, you'll tell her and everyone else at the same time. If there's too much objection to your idea, you'll need to come up with a new one."

Aahmes frowned. Still, this idea gripped him. He felt certain that once he presented it—in front of all the Shadowers, no less—she would not feel she could back down from it. If she did, it would show beyond any doubt that he was matchless.

"I can be ready to tell her the thievery task this night," he said.

Dar studied him, his brown eyes narrowed. Then he gave a sharp nod.

"Well then, if she tells me herself that she agrees to having you design the Trial, tonight it is. After the evening meal."

He turned back to his desk, a clear dismissal, and Aahmes left.

He strode back down the hall to the stairs, defying the fatigue that dogged his heels after too little sleep so far this day. He had a few candle-marks until the evening meal. He should have time to at least start finding out what the rout was up to.

Might others in the city be involved, too?

That could get ugly.

~ ~ ~

After he grabbed a few vikls and korz—the silver and copper coins of the Six Realms—from his stash in his room, Aahmes went in search of one of the messenger children that haunted Rhadanthus' streets hoping to run errands for coins to be able to eat. A few streets away from Shadow Keep, Aahmes found a girl several winters younger than himself who was dressed in the city-required clothing that signified a messenger – clothing that all matched in color.

Hers was a dusty brown several shades lighter than her red-brown skin and the dark-brown hair that peeked out from under her cap. The clothes hung on her, too large for her skinny frame. She clearly hoped for errands to run, leaning toward each person who passed with a questioning expression. She greeted Aahmes with a warm smile when he stopped in front of her.

"Got a message yeh need run to someone, sir?" she said. "I'll get it done before yeh have time to wonder where I been."

Aahmes matched her smile. "That I do, if you don't mind dealing with Ezeor's rout."

"Ezeor?" the girl repeated, her expression confused. "I don't...wait! Yeh mean Clodarn's rout." She scrunched up her face, showing her opinion of them. "Clodarn took it over when his da died. Couple years back. I can deal with 'em. I've run errands to 'em before."

Aahmes hid his surprise. He had not heard that the

rout's leader had died. He also had not known that the man had a son. Ezeor had been only a little more than twice Aahmes' age, best he could tell. He returned his attention to the girl.

"Good. This'll be an easy one. Find one of them, doesn't matter which, and tell them Aahmes wants to meet to talk. And bring back whatever message they have as answer."

"'Aahmes wants to meet to talk'," the girl repeated. "Got it. Shouldn't take more than half a candle-mark to get it to one of 'em. Prob'ly less. Where'll I find yeh to bring the answer?"

"You know the Broken Door Tavern?" When she nodded, he continued. "Find me there. And there'll be another one of these for you when you do, whether or not there's a return message." He handed her a vikl.

Her eyes widened at the sight of the silver coin and so did her smile. "Thank yeh! I'll be there!" She ran off.

The Broken Door Tavern was in the same ring of the city as the Keep but in the eastern part of Rhadanthus. With a few shortcuts, Aahmes made it there in good time. The girl would likely not be there for at least another quarter candle-mark he estimated, so he took the opportunity to climb to the top of the city wall. From there he studied the walled stronghold that sat outside the city. It belonged to Chendrukhar, a man with the Power that many called magic.

Yes, that should be such a challenging Trial for her that she would fail and find herself out of the guild. With a smug smile, he headed to the tavern to await his messenger.

The tavern's owner Feona greeted him with the smile that was only for him. "There you are, lover. Haven't seen you in too many days."

Aahmes paused halfway across the room to admire her, as he often did when he visited her there. Her red-tinted lips, curved in that smile, stood out against her beautiful dark skin. She was perhaps a couple of winters older than him and dressed in a simple shirt tucked into a long skirt – her usual attire when running her tavern. She wore her black hair in many thin braids that reached below her shoulders. He met her smile with one of his own.

She poured a drink for him and set it on the counter. When he sat on the stool there, she leaned toward him to run her fingers along his jaw to his lips.

"Been so elseways busy you didn't have time to visit me?" She gave him a dramatic pout.

With a gentle touch, he moved her fingers from his lips so he could take a long drink. Then he smiled at her. "You know how it is," he said. "How's the tavern doing?"

She looked around the empty room with a grin. "Close to too busy, though you can't tell this time o' day. But tonight'll be roaring. Could use another pair of hands or two to keep up with it all, if you know anyone who's needing some work."

Aahmes grinned. Shadowers took care of their own, even those they did not like. So if Namid failed her Trial….

"I might know someone," he told Feona. "If so, I'll make sure to send her your direction. Could be a few days, though."

She patted his cheek. "I'll muddle through. Come visit again after hours, if you've a mind to."

He leaned close and twined one of her thin braids around his fingers. "I'll be sure to come see you."

She brushed her fingers across his cheek, but her gaze went beyond him, to something behind him.

"What can I do for you, dearie?" she said.

Aahmes looked over his shoulder and spotted the messenger girl hovering at the edge of the doorway. "She's got something for me," he told Feona and took his drink to a table by the door, waving for the girl to join him.

With a surprised expression, she did and balanced on the edge of her chair.

Feona brought her a mug of water and left them to talk.

After the girl took a long drink, she smiled at Aahmes. "Thank yeh. That tastes good. Delivered the message. And I got the answer for yeh. 'Meet tonight, usual place, two candle-marks after sundown', they said to tell yeh." She took another drink.

Aahmes handed her the promised vikl. "You have my thanks," he said. "Who did you talk to?"

"Don't know his name. Big man, bigger than yeh. But he had to talk with someone else to get the answer."

Aahmes nodded.

The girl finished her water in a gulp and hopped to her feet. "Need anything else?"

When he shook his head, she dashed off, calling back that he should remember her next time he did.

While Feona continued working to get the place ready for the nighttime crowd, Aahmes finished his own drink. With a wave to her, he took the mug into the kitchen and left it in a bucket of soapy water, then headed back to Shadow Keep, taking a winding route, as always, to do his part to help keep the place's location a secret.

Maybe he would even have time to get a little sleep before the evening meal and his nighttime activities.

He groaned to himself when Dar caught him as he climbed the stairs to his room.

"Not going to keep you," Dar said. "Just letting you know Namid has confirmed that you'll design her Trial. And agreed to having the announcement this evening. You sure you're ready?"

"Yeah," Aahmes mumbled around a stifled yawn.

Dar clapped him on the shoulder. "Then go get your rest. These next days'll keep you busy, I think."

CHAPTER 4

Aahmes barely noticed the food and wine at the noisy evening meal, distracted as he was with wondering about the rout and deciding on the final details of Namid's Trial. His idea for her Trial pleased him. He hoped she would feel properly goaded by the challenge it presented, would so strongly feel the need to prove that she *could* do this that she would not think of requiring a different task.

And when she failed at it, that would be the end of that. He would nudge her toward work at the tavern and she would no longer be of any concern. That would be one trouble taken care of.

Aahmes' table mates chattered about Namid's readiness for her Trial and made various wagers on it. Aahmes declined to join in the wagers but had to smile that they already knew she would be starting her Trial. Dar had not yet announced it, but it seemed everyone in this building of skilled skulkers already knew it.

When most had finished their meals, Dar rose to his feet and pounded on the table to get everyone's attention. In the ensuing silence, he briefly admonished Zwena and Orran for going off-task during their most recent job, then announced Namid's successful completion of her apprenticeship and readiness for her Trial.

Aahmes did not join in the shouts of approval that followed, but when Dar urged Namid to stand, he did smirk, thinking of what her reaction would be when she heard what he set as her task for her Trial.

After the room quieted again, Dar reminded everyone of the two parts of the Trial, then told them that Aahmes would design both aspects.

Aahmes stood and gave the room at large a smug bow. He turned his gaze to Namid, who stood three tables away. He could not contain his satisfied grin at her apprehensive expression.

He raised his voice to be heard over the mutters of the other Shadowers. "To complete your Trial, beyond your weapons-work—which will be against me—your task is to steal and deliver to us the Star of Corentris."

His grin widened at the reaction to his announcement. Namid gaped at him and the room exploded into confusion. All that he could have hoped for when the idea had come to him.

The Star of Corentris—a star-shaped statue made of some rare, silvery metal—represented the type of theft most of those there dreamed of accomplishing, a theft well beyond all but the most accomplished of them. And even those Shadowers might have difficulties with this theft. It belonged to the mage Chendrukhar, who kept it in his stronghold outside the city, where he ofttimes flaunted it for high-ranking guests, or so word had it.

From across the hall, Jaikrein shouted a dispute. Dar pounded the table again for quiet so everyone could hear her dispute.

Aahmes was unsurprised when Jaikrein claimed that the theft could not be done. Certainly, *she* would not be able to accomplish such a theft, nor would most of the others. But then she reminded everyone that it must be something the Trial's designer could do alone and claimed that even *he* could not do it.

Aahmes worked to keep his expression impassive but cursed to himself as the mutters seemed to agree. He *did* remember Dar saying something like that, didn't he? He looked from Jaikrein's challenging gaze to Namid. She, in turn, was looking at Dar, who agreed the dispute had validity and told Aahmes to come up with another test.

What else could he come up with? This had seemed such a perfect idea that he had not even considered any other task.

Then Namid shouted, "Wait!" and asked how long she would have to accomplish the task.

Aahmes suppressed his triumphant smile. He had been almost certain that she would not back down from this task of his that, in essence, amounted to a dare. He threw out the suggestion of one night beyond the current one, the shortest amount of time he had considered offering, to see what she would make of it.

Still Jaikrein persisted in disputing.

Why couldn't she just *stop*? He almost had Namid....

"I've already proven myself. Are you casting question on my abilities?" Aahmes rested his hand on the hilt of one of his daggers and scowled at his fellows to remind them of who they were dealing with, of his skill with both thievery and daggers.

Silence spread as his message sank in. Even Jaikrein looked at least a little cowed. Aahmes smiled to himself, then let the smile out as a vicious grin directed at Namid, while he directed his next words to everyone, offering to make her Trial truly difficult by grabbing the statue first himself, leaving her to try to steal something that had already been stolen once before. And recently.

Of course that would make her task that much more difficult, if not impossible. The muttering increased after he spoke.

Namid ignored his flippant offer and instead argued that the time was too short for the whole Trial.

"I assume you want the weapons-work in the midst of all this?" she said.

He had already decided on that – make the whole thing that much harder. He nodded.

She acted unsurprised and suggested two nights beyond the current one for completing the task of stealing the Star. Then she gave him an expectant look.

He considered that, well aware of everyone's intent attention.

"You're accepting?" Dar said to her, his voice and expression both incredulous.

Namid held up her hand, forestalling him. "Would you give me this long?" she said to Aahmes.

Aahmes studied her. What were her intentions? Another day should not be much help to her, he decided, so he shrugged and agreed, with an unconcerned grin.

The mutters started again and Namid raised her voice over them to propose an alteration to the terms of the Trial. "I'll agree to get the Star of Corentris before the third dawn hence, if…."

After a pause to look around the room, she continued, "If Aahmes agrees to return it afterward."

"Return it?" someone shouted.

Jaikrein shouted back, "Yes, return it. We all know it can't be kept from its owner longer than half a day without him learnin' its exact location. And then he'd be comin' for it!"

Aahmes, too, had heard that tale about the statue. He wondered if anyone knew the truth of it. Perhaps the tale had been told so many times that people took it for fact, whether or not it was really true.

Aahmes watched Dar and Namid exchange looks. Dar did not look happy.

"That's my counter. If my *most worthy* Trial overseer accepts my conditions, then I accept his test," Namid said over the continuing whispers and rustles. From her mock bow, Aahmes easily recognized her disdain for what they both knew he was trying to set her up for.

Aahmes frowned at her, glanced around the room, then agreed. "By the third dawn from now, you'll put the Star of Corentris into my hands."

Namid agreed then, too. By guild custom, that sealed the terms of her Trial.

Everyone began talking again, louder than before. Ignoring the glares he gathered, Aahmes pushed his way through Namid's supporters as they crowded around her.

He leaned close to Namid when he reached her, dropping his voice almost to a whisper. "I agreed only because I know I'll not be called on to return the Star."

"We'll see," she said, giving him a superior, irritating look.

"Yes, we shall see. And you'll face me tomorrow after the evening meal for the weapons-work part of your Trial." He laughed while he walked away.

Partway up the stairs from the main floor, Aahmes heard running footsteps behind him. He turned to see who it was and groaned to himself.

Not Macai. Not right then. Aahmes wanted to focus on the coming meeting with the rout.

Still he waited for the other to catch up to him. The lanky man with his crooked nose and scraggly, pale yellow hair and whiskers stood close to a head shorter than Aahmes, and that was when he did not stand a step lower than him as he did then. Aahmes hoped that Macai had not come to encourage him in one of the elaborate schemes the older Shadower was known for, the schemes that most often ended with Macai drawing the Warders' attention.

"Your first Trial designing," Macai greeted him. "It's my congratulations I'm offering you."

"My thanks," Aahmes said and turned to try to make his escape up the stairs. But Macai grabbed his arm, preventing that.

"Bide a moment. I've some advice for you, some ideas

to help you make a success of this. About those little extra difficulties that a Trial overseer can add…." He then treated Aahmes to one of his notorious, lengthy explanations, detailing all sorts of challenges that Aahmes could add to Namid's Trial.

Aahmes tried to follow his convoluted description – there was always a chance Macai might offer something that would be useful, in a simplified form. But with his honest lack of interest in Macai's schemes, Aahmes found his mind wandering.

After trying several times to interrupt the other man, Aahmes finally managed to break into Macai's improbable description of ways to use a ribbon and a pastry as a challenge for Namid.

"I'm sure that would be very…different," Aahmes said. "I'm all set, though. My thanks for the information. Say, here's an idea. I'm sure young Namid would benefit from your superior knowledge of schemes. Why not go talk with her?"

Macai glowered at being interrupted, but his expression brightened at Aahmes' suggestion.

"Aye, indeed. You have the right of it. I'll do just that. I know I can offer her some fine ideas." He scurried back down the stairs.

Aahmes sighed, then grinned. Macai's advice could reasonably be considered a challenge a Shadower would often face.

So that made *one* of the extra difficulties.

Chapter 5

Unable to get his thoughts in any good order, Aahmes at least managed to gather and prepare the weapons he wanted to take before he needed to go meet with the rout. Shadow Keep was quiet when he left – most of the others had gone out already on various tasks and thefts.

The 'usual place' that Aahmes was supposed to meet the rout was an abandoned building somewhat south of the Keep, in the area the rout claimed as its own. Other bands claimed various other parts of the city, with hostilities where one claim overlapped another. The Shadowers claimed no specific area and did not recognize the rascals' claims. They went where they wished.

Aahmes arrived early and perched atop the wall of the building across the street to wait – its wood roof had collapsed sometime in the past. His gray cloak helped him blend in with the broken stones and he crouched motionless, settled in his chosen spot. Someone from the rout should arrive soon enough.

After long enough that his feet grew chilled within his boots, a sensation of being watched crept over him. He slowly turned, peering into the moonlit night and spotted a figure easing along the street toward him. When it was closer, it pushed back its hood and looked up at him. He hid his grimace – he had hoped it would be anyone but her.

"Phrae," he greeted her and hopped down from his perch.

"Aahmes." She nodded to him and turned back the way she had come. "This way," she said over a shoulder.

"We're not meeting in the house?" He waved a hand at the ruined building on the other side of the street.

"No. Someplace less open."

Aahmes frowned but followed her. Under cover of his cloak he fingered his daggers, checking that all were secure in their spots around his body. He still had that sensation of being watched but did not see anyone lurking in the night.

They walked perhaps a quarter candle-mark before Phrae led the way into another abandoned building, through the front room and into one in back. She stepped around and under the broken remnants of a staircase that led up and headed down stone stairs that led into the ground.

Aahmes paused at the top and peered into the dark hole. "What's this?"

"The rout leader would speak wi' yeh hisself. Got this nice little hidey hole to use."

Phrae descended a couple more steps then opened a lantern that hung on the wall and lifted it down.

She glanced back at Aahmes, her expression expectant in the lantern's light.

With a glower, Aahmes followed her.

At the bottom of the stairs they turned left and followed a narrow rock tunnel for several paces, then turned right into a small room. The walls of both the tunnel and room were rough-hewn, more like a cave than some sort of cellar. A bright lantern lit the room. Phrae shuttered the lantern she carried and took a place along the wall.

Aahmes followed her into the room, a hand on the hilt of one of his daggers. Berz stood against the wall across the room, next to another opening. The third person in the room was a man about Aahmes' age, so he guessed. The stranger's hair and skin were both brown, his hair a shade or two lighter than Berz's. His clothes were a better quality than those of the other rout members, a bit better than Aahmes' even. He gazed at Aahmes with a speculative expression.

"I'm Clodarn, now leader of this rout. I'm glad you came to meet with me," he said.

"I didn't know Ezeor had children," Aahmes said.

Clodarn's smile was toothy. "There's just me. Da pretty much kept me hidden. But don't mistake, he taught me well."

Aahmes waved a hand at the other two rout members in the room. "If you can keep these in line, I don't doubt it. So what do you want with me?"

Clodarn studied Aahmes long enough to make him edgy. "We want you to return," he said finally. "Mix with us again, especially now that we're a true rout."

Aahmes grinned at the snort that came from Phrae's direction. "Seems not all of you really want me to mix with you again. And I don't see that happening anyway."

In a sudden change of mood, Clodarn laughed. "We can deal with that later. For now, you need to do something for us."

With an expectant look, he waited for Aahmes to ask. The silence stretched as Aahmes outwaited him.

"Fine," Clodarn said with a frown. "Your precious Shadowers have something we need. You need to steal it from them and bring it to us."

Aahmes folded his arms and stared at him long enough that the other man fidgeted.

"I *need* to do this?" Aahmes sneered, then laughed. "Your rout isn't good enough to steal this thing on their own."

Clodarn glared at him. "Not from your wretched Shadow Keep," he admitted. "But there's more. You can't just ask for the item, you can't tell anyone about it. Our patron requires complete secrecy."

Aahmes quirked an eyebrow at him. "Patron? Since when did a band like this work for some *patron*?"

"Since it became worth our while." Clodarn turned away but glanced back at him over a shoulder. "He's gathered several routs to work for him. I think he means to gather them all. We'll become quite important in Rhadanthus."

Aahmes kept his expression bland but squirmed inside. This could get bad for the Shadowers.

"I still don't see that I *need* to do this. Or would want to," he said and turned toward the stairway out.

"You're the best. You always were the best thief in any rout."

Aahmes waved off his comment, putting up a show of indifference. He did not really mind Dar using his pride to motivate him, but he had no intention of letting any rascals use it to get him to do what they wanted. "Get someone else if you need the thing so badly."

"We've got someone in that group of yours. But they can't manage it."

Aahmes glowered at that. Dar would need to know that information. He hesitated. If he agreed, maybe he could find out the rat's identity.

"Be a shame. Aahms, if somethin' bad happened t' that pretty little sister yeh've got," Berz spoke up. "Especially when she's so close t' becomin' a *real* Shadower."

Aahmes scowled and turned back. "She's not my sister."

Berz snorted. "I've seen her. Yeh look 'nuff alike t' maybe be twins even."

"Really?" Aahmes sneered. "I'd never noticed that. My thanks for pointing that out. She's *not* my sister. What might happen to her is no concern of mine."

Berz gave him a predatory grin. "Sure. Tell yerself that."

Aahmes stalked toward him, dagger out. "We're not related. And don't spread any tales that we are."

Berz's eyes widened and he held up his hands in a warding gesture. "All right. Fine. Settle, man."

"If you don't do what we need, our *friend* within the Shadowers will rip them apart," Clodarn said, "from the inside. Starting with that item, which, if discovered with your group, will tear away the benefits of any favors you've built over the years with the city's powerful. Our patron will have us wreck your precious Shadowers all around you, even give out the secret of where you hole up. So you see, it benefits you, and your Shadowers both, to get the item away."

Aahmes glared at him. This just kept getting worse. "And what is this item?"

Clodarn smiled. "It's an amber-colored shawl. Silk. With elaborate embroidery in gold thread."

"A *shawl?*"

The rout leader grinned at his surprise and nodded. "It belongs to a certain highly placed noble. Her husband gifted it to her and has been distressed that she has not worn it recently."

"Your patron wants to get some noble's *shawl* back to her?" Aahmes said, his expression incredulous.

Clodarn laughed. "Not exactly. You don't need the details. You just need to get us that shawl. And don't tell any of your Shadower friends. Our hidden *friend* will be watching to make sure you keep the secret."

Aahmes peered at the three rout members. He already had an idea about where the shawl might be, so that part should be easy. But to steal from the Shadowers was a betrayal, even if it was only a piece of clothing. Sure, the Shadowers often played pranks on each other by pilfering something, then usually hiding it. But nothing in earnest.

They did *not* steal from each other.

Still, if he could figure out who the rout had within the guild, then he could explain everything to Dar. Besides, it was Dar who had asked him to find out what the rout was up to in the first place.

"Fine." Aahmes worked to give the impression that he felt intimidated by the accumulation of their threats. "I'll get this shawl for you. And I won't tell any of my Shadower friends."

He gave the rout members a sidelong look. "So who do you have hidden in the Shadowers, anyway?"

Phrae laughed. "Never yeh mind that. Yeh're not needin' to know who it is."

Clodarn sauntered to the other doorway and stretched a hand out toward Phrae. "I knew you'd see it our way," he said over his shoulder to Aahmes. "Can you get us the shawl this night?"

Aahmes shook his head. "Very doubtful. I *do* have other things I need to be doing."

"Tomorrow then." Clodarn said with a nod as Phrae joined him. They left the room together, each with an arm wrapped around the other's waist.

"More likely the next day," Aahmes called after them.

Then he and Berz exchanged glowers.

"I wouldn't mind if yeh didn't get it," Berz whispered. "Be great t' be able t' tear yer Shadowers down. And extra nice t' take yeh with them."

With a shake of his head, Aahmes left him in the underground hideaway. He noted the place's location—one street north of the old long-abandoned Bigge Smithy—then used all his skills to remain unseen while he took himself away. No sensation of any watchers followed him. As he moved through the city's shadows, he wondered what particular grievance Berz seemed to have with the guild.

~ ~ ~

Aahmes did not hurry to cross the city to Feona's tavern. She would be busy for some time yet and a restlessness dogged him. His path took him near the inner rings of the city, the wealthy city center, and back out again. In spite of the cold, plenty of people wandered the streets near the center, giving him plenty of opportunities to snatch some coin pouches. He emptied out the coins into his own pouch and left the empty pouches scattered about in his wake, dropped in shadowed corners.

Who among the Shadowers might be mixed with the rout? There weren't many newer members and of those, he could think of none who would do something like that. He frowned when he remembered Berz's mention of that tyro. Could it maybe be her?

After giving that some consideration, he decided it was unlikely, at best. As if his musings had summoned her, Aahmes spotted the younger Shadower in the gloom across from the Wayfarers Inn. Torches on the building's front wall lit the empty open yard between the tyro and the inn's door. Aahmes eased back into the shadows himself and watched Namid study the inn, then pull her cloak close and put up her hood before she entered the building.

What could she possibly be doing there?

He saw two City Warders further down the street watch her enter. After they returned to their conversation, an idea came to him. Time for Namid to encounter another challenge that full guild members often ran into.

But first, he needed a guise.

Aahmes located the inn's stables nearby. He hurried to them and inside through a small door at the back, keeping out of sight of the Warders. Within, he found two stablehands asleep in one stall and a few wagons and horses elsewhere. Looked like probably only one or two caravans there this early in the season.

He grabbed a blanket that smelled horsey enough and wrapped it around himself, pushing his hood down to hide it with his cloak beneath the blanket. With a grimace, he next deliberately stepped in some manure that the stablehands had not cleaned up yet. Not like he hadn't had the stuff on his boots before.

After he pulled his hair forward to hang over his eyes and help obscure his features, he hurried out the front door and made a show of looking around then spotting the Warders. With a calculated limp, he scuttled to them.

"Ah, good it is I've found yeh, good Warders." Aahmes pitched his voice higher than its normal tone. "Not wantin' to make any trouble, but I'm pretty sure I seen someone who don' belong, a thief prob'ly, maybe even one o' them Shadowers, they're called, ain't they?"

That caught the Warders' attention.

"Hiding in the stable?" one said as he dropped a hand to the hilt of his sword. The other wrinkled her nose when Aahmes edged close.

"Ah, no, good Warders, not there." Aahmes pointed toward the inn. "Just over there. Watchin' the inn earlier, by the looks o' it. Maybe plannin' somethin' against the guests. Come t' think on it, I seen them hangin' around earlier, talkin' to some others. One said somethin' about gettin' away wi' it like with that Inner Ring affair back afore last winter."

"That person we saw go in," said the Warder who had wrinkled her nose. The two Warders exchanged glances and Aahmes hid his smile. "Get the Warders from the next street," the woman told her companion. As he ran off, she turned back to Aahmes.

"Better get yourself back to your horses. Stay safe hidden there until we're done," she told him.

Aahmes bowed several times as he backed toward the stable. "Aye, that I will. Thank yeh."

"You there. Whatcha playin' at?" a voice called from behind Aahmes.

With a sinking feeling, he glanced over his shoulder. One of the stablehands stood in the open door to the stable. He pointed at Aahmes.

"Thief!"

Cursing, Aahmes ducked when the Warder grabbed for him. She got a handful of the blanket.

Still cursing, he twisted and squirmed until he freed himself from the blanket. He ran off into the darkness, leaving the Warder holding the blanket and shouting for more Warders. The stablehand added his shouts to hers.

CHAPTER 6

Well away from the inn before more Warders arrived, Aahmes paused several streets over. He had no desire to visit Feona with manure on his boots. He could find one of the city's wells to rinse them, but that might not be enough. And he did not like the idea of icy water soaking his boots in the cold night, either. A sniff of his shirt and cloak told him he smelled like horse, too. He did not mind, but she might.

Aahmes looked around. He was not too far from Carssi's Baths, and he had plenty of coins with him. Why not stop in and get cleaned up? Maybe take some time to get his thoughts in order about this rout affair, too.

The boy at the door to Carssi's Baths recognized him – he tried to stop by whenever he could to enjoy the luxury of the warm pools. Aahmes handed over the coins to get all of his clothing cleaned and for a pool to himself. From the number of guests already there, with more entering behind him, the place seemed headed for a busy night.

He shed his boots and clothes in one of the tiny changing rooms and hung them from a hook on the wall. Nice to not have to clean them himself for a change.

Aahmes wrapped a towel around his waist, grabbed the bundle that held all his weapons and headed to the pool the boy had indicated for him.

Set in the area for people not interested in the more intimate goings-on behind the screens, his pool was larger than he expected and grouped with two other pools filled with lounging people who talked and laughed together. A couple of them gave him half waves of casual greeting when he stopped at the third pool.

He found a tray already there at the edge, with a glass of wine waiting for him. Aahmes slipped into the warm water with a sigh, leaving his weapons, with his towel covering them, next to the tray. Murky with the scented extracts Carssi liked to put in the pools, the water hid anything beneath the surface. Aahmes smelled no strong scent from his pool, not that he would have objected if he had. He planned no further thievery this night. He seated himself on the wide ledge that sat several handspans beneath the water's surface and served as both step and seat.

Aahmes took a sip of his wine and slouched, sliding further into the pool. A minstrel strolled past, playing some sweet tune on his lute. Aahmes sighed again in pleasure as the heat from the water soaked through him. He could get used to this.

He let his thoughts drift and soon they turned to his task for the rout. They must have been offered a lot to convince them to work for someone else. And what about this patron? Who could it be? Some other snooty noble who wanted to make trouble in their own elite circle, he imagined.

But a shawl? What had prompted someone to bring back a shawl? Assuming that was how it got to Shadow Keep. Must be.

So, assuming it *was* there, it must be stashed somewhere in Keizha's two rooms beneath the Keep's kitchen area. There she kept a great variety of things they could use for a guise, when they needed one. Including a shawl, Aahmes supposed.

Why did the rout want it so quickly? Aahmes shrugged and took another sip of wine. Tomorrow would be soon enough. Easier to get the thing anyway during the day when so many of the Shadowers preferred to sleep.

He started to doze. He fought it at first, then decided why not? He had time; he had paid well for his time here at the Baths so no one would object. And he would be that much more rested for his visit with Feona later.

He settled himself lower in his pool, submerged to his shoulders, and sipped his wine.

A sound like a mix of a gasp and growl drew his attention. He looked up to find Namid standing near the other edge of his pool. She wore one of the short bathing shifts the place provided if a person wanted. Even from across the pool, he smelled the noxious odor that wafted off her. Had she rolled in a garbage pile? That explained her presence. So much for having the pool to himself. Still, this could be entertaining.

He grinned at her and raised his glass in greeting.

"I see you got away." He kept his voice low so no one in the other pools would be able to make out his words. With a show of wrinkling his nose, he added, "And I can see—or smell, rather—why you've decided to stop in here. Although time's passing."

She started to say something, then stopped herself. Grabbing a small cleaning cloth and tiny piece of soap from a nearby bench, she slipped into the pool and scrubbed vigorously.

Aahmes grinned to himself. It looked like she wanted to get away again as soon as she could manage. He had no objection – he'd like her to be away and leave him in peace.

When she accused him of sending the Warders after her, keeping her voice quiet too, he shrugged, hoping to rile her with his indifference.

"I, my dear young tyro?" he said as he shifted along the side of the pool so her soapy water ran past him to the outlet. He claimed he only knew that the Warders had heard that someone was lurking about the inn, someone who had been involved in the Inner Ring affair.

With a pointed look for him, she implied that *he* had been neck deep in that mess.

Of course he said he had no idea what she was talking about. She did not need to know that she had guessed correctly. With another shrug, he sipped his wine again. Maybe he needed to goad her more to get her out of his pool.

"You must be so proud of yourself," he taunted. "Having already worked out exactly how to accomplish your task so you can take time to linger here and wash up. What's next? A visit to one of those fancy-dress shops to get yourself a pretty gown? Maybe you'd better wait until after you've failed your Trial and see if you can get a new gown in your new position as some lady's assistant. Or, no, server in some tavern, more likely." Would not hurt to plant the idea in her head. She would need it later, he was sure. He chuckled deliberately.

She glared at him before she turned her back and hurried her washing.

He leaned back with both arms stretched out to the sides along the rim of the pool, head tilted back, and smiled to himself. He let his eyes drift almost closed and just watched her through the barest slits.

After she rinsed off the soap, she glanced over her shoulder at him and seemed to study him. Her expression changed. Looked like she wanted to do something. He tried not to tense as he wondered if she was going to attack him.

But she turned away again and sniffed her arm and hair. Must be checking to see if the stench was gone.

"I'll finish some other time…when they've cleared the waters of all the scum," she tossed back over her shoulder as she climbed from the pool.

Aahmes laughed, more for effect than because he found her comment amusing. He watched her head for the changing rooms and kept watching until she emerged, dressed in her normal clothes again, and left the building.

So she had at least passed the challenge of Warders looking for her. Not without some trouble, he guessed, from her manner, and the smell, of course. Good!

He wondered if her plans to accomplish her main task had been colored by Macai's input. He hoped so.

~ ~ ~

After a pleasurable time spent with Feona, with her tavern closed for the night, Aahmes ambled back to Shadow Keep. The sun had risen but did little to warm the chill air. He took an even more convoluted path than usual, worried about Clodarn's threat to expose the place's location, worried about anyone following him although he felt no sense of being watched.

He found something to eat in the kitchen and, when no one was in the room to see him leave, he headed downstairs to Keizha's underground rooms.

He tapped on the door. When there was no answer, he eased it open and peered within.

On the far side of the room, Keizha lay asleep on her narrow bed. Aahmes watched her several long breaths-of-time. After he felt sure she really slept, he edged into the room and eased the door closed behind him.

Shelves filled much of the room, along with tables and trunks, all of which held a variety of items, mostly clothing of various sizes, colors and styles. Aahmes peered around the room, looking for anything that resembled the shawl that had been described to him. But after he scrutinized the collection, he could not even tell how Keizha had it organized. Whenever he had needed something before, he had just asked, and she had gone right to it. He might have to figure a way to do that again.

With silent steps, he slipped into her second room, and found the same thing there. He might search for candle-marks and still not locate this shawl. And that assumed she did not wake and catch him.

He turned slowly to look again to make certain he had not missed something obvious and spotted something at the bottom of a stack on a high shelf. The fabric looked browner than the orange-yellow he considered amber but seemed to have embroidery. Maybe that was it.

He reached up and tugged at the folded cloth, hoping to pull it from beneath the others stacked atop it. But it was stuck.

He tried sliding a hand atop the piece he wanted and under the rest and that seemed to loosen the stack some. So he pulled harder on the amber-brown cloth.

"Lookin' like you could use oh-so-much help there, yes?"

Aahmes started at the sound of Keizha's voice right behind him. How had he not heard her approach? He flailed his arms to keep his balance, then cringed as the entire stack of clothing fell on him.

He smoothed out his scowl and turned to face Keizha's laughter.

The small, older Shadower—the top of her head did not reach his shoulder—stood not an armlength behind him. Her laughter faded, but she still grinned at him, her smooth golden-brown skin and dark, dark eyes crinkled with her mirth. Her normally sleek, chin-length white hair was rumpled from sleep.

With a hint of a glare for Aahmes, she bent to gather the various items of clothing strewn around him. He hurried to help her.

"Why not ask for what you're wantin'?" she said as they worked to fold the clothing and stack it on a nearby table.

"I didn't want to disturb you," Aahmes said.

She snorted. "I'm sure that's oh-so-right, in more ways

than one. Still, we Shadowers do like our secrets."

Aahmes frowned and did not respond to that.

After they finished stacking everything else on the table, more or less neatly, Keizha held up the item Aahmes had been after. He saw it was a fancy shirt, embroidered, but no shawl.

"Mighty pretty, this is," Keizha commented and measured it against Aahmes' shoulders. "Not a good fit for you, though. Plannin' on sneakin' int' one of the elites' fancy gatherin's?"

Aahmes shrugged. "Thinking of some possibilities."

She snorted again. "You're needin' t' work on your lies a bit there. Still, you're young. So what is it you're really wantin'?"

Aahmes glanced around. No one else about and surely Keizha would not be the rout's sneak. Still….

Although, maybe he could come at it sideways….

"Something I've wondered. Why would any of us steal clothing? I know we use these pieces for guises when we need, but otherwise they're not worth much of anything."

Keizha laughed. "Odd t' come in now with a question like that," she said. "But better. We don't need t' now, but in times past we had little enough that clothes were almost as worthwhile as the gems and gold coins you grab. And, as you said, they're great for guises." She leaned close and lowered her voice. "And every so often, some clothes are oh-so-worthwhile. Say somethin' made of the finest cloth. Or with precious gems attached."

Her expression was expectant.

"Do we have anything like that right now?"

"Other than this shirt, not down here. Problem with those things is they can be too distinctive. Hard t' sell and dangerous t' use as guises. Usually take them apart and use the pieces somehow."

Aahmes tried to hide his disappointment at that.

Keizha leaned closer, her voice not much more than a whisper. "Now sometimes, someone might keep such a thing for themselves. Because they like it. Might be whatever you're after is one of those items."

Aahmes gave her a sharp look but she just smiled back at him and urged him back to the door.

"On your way now, so I can get back t' my sleepin'."

With a silent sigh, he let her ease him back out her door. She closed it behind him.

Interesting that it might be in some Shadower's possession. Could he think of a good-enough story to explain why he would be asking about a shawl?

CHAPTER 7

As he trudged up the stairs to his room, Aahmes looked forward to falling into his bed. His time in the pool and with Feona had relaxed him, but he needed more real sleep.

"Good, you're back."

Aahmes groaned at the sound of Dar's voice. The guild leader stood on the second-floor landing, waiting for him.

When Aahmes looked at him as he climbed the last few steps, Dar frowned. "You look a bit ragged. Won't keep you long."

He led the way into his office and closed the door. Then he stepped to the far wall and beckoned Aahmes close.

"What've you found out? You did meet with the rout last night, didn't you?"

Aahmes nodded and worked to pull his sluggish thoughts together. "It's definite they want me to return to them," he offered first, to give himself more time to decide what else to share.

Dar studied him. "Still sure you wouldn't do that?" he said eventually.

"Completely," Aahmes said without hesitation. "But there's more." He lowered his voice to a whisper. In spite of what Clodarn had threatened, Dar needed to know this. "Sounds like they're trying to join together with others – and seems more bands of rascals are calling themselves routs now. Seems to be someone pulling them all together for some reason."

"To challenge us?"

"I don't know. Might be."

"Bad enough I'd suspected your old rout of trying to move in on us, but all of them working together…that could be real trouble."

Aahmes nodded. Should he mention the possibility that someone from the rout was in the Shadowers? And the threat to expose the Keep's location? Dar should know, but Aahmes knew how voices carried through the walls, even with them standing as far away as possible from walls shared with other spaces within the Keep. Or he could keep that information to himself and perhaps find out who it was on his own.

Aahmes raked a hand back through his hair. Neither choice sounded good.

"Anything else?" Dar prompted.

"We didn't talk long. I'm supposed to meet with them again."

Dar nodded. "Do so. If you need to, do you think you can act like you *do* want to mix with them again? If it will get us more information?"

"Maybe."

Dar clapped him on the shoulder. "Try. Now, what have you to say about the progress of Namid's Trial? I'm sure you've been keeping track of her."

"Am I supposed to be?"

Dar chuckled. "It's not required, but generally a good idea. Make sure things don't get out of hand."

"Hmm. Well, she managed to evade some Warders who were hunting for Shadowers. And Macai eagerly shared his thoughts with her. Plots and schemes to succeed at her task, I'd wager."

Dar peered at him. "She evaded some Warders, did she? That's a risky extra challenge to add. And you set Macai on her, too?" Dar's expression held more than a hint of disapproval.

Aahmes shrugged.

"Anything else?"

"I'd like to do her weapons-work Trial after the evening meal today," Aahmes said. "Or did I already tell you that?"

"You didn't."

"A straight-forward bout with daggers," Aahmes said. "Maybe a choice of blades."

Dar nodded. "I'll make the arrangements for the weapons and judges."

When Aahmes yawned, Dar guided the younger man toward the door. "And I'll let you get some sleep. You'll no doubt want to be alert and ready this evening."

With a hint of a scowl, Aahmes nodded then took himself to his own room and bed.

~ ~ ~

After several candle-marks of unsatisfactory dozing, Aahmes decided he might as well just get up. A quick visit to the kitchen got him something to eat, and a glare from the Shadower assigned to meal preparation when he snatched the food. Then he roamed the Keep while he ate.

Few Shadowers were in the upper levels, so he poked into rooms looking for any sign of the shawl, or anything that might connect someone to the rout. Although he had no idea what the latter might be.

He did locate several stashes in the various rooms, but he found no amber-colored shawl. Aahmes took care to leave everything the way he found it and took nothing except some nice secrets to hold to himself.

While he worked his way through the Keep, from time to time he heard a footstep somewhere behind him, or a door close nearby. But every time he looked, he saw no one. The rout member watching him? Or his imagination getting the better of him? He could not decide which.

After he finished looking through the upper levels of the Keep, including his roommate's half of their shared room, Aahmes debated the merits versus the hazards of looking through rooms on the Keep's second floor: the floor where those of the highest rank in the Shadowers had their rooms.

His steps slowed on the stairway as he approached that floor. It could be a lot of trouble if any of them caught him. And it was more probable that he *would* be caught than it had been on the upper floors.

Still undecided, he rounded the corner from the bottom of the staircase into the main hallway and smacked into Aerill. Without thinking he jumped back and had a dagger half drawn before he realized who it was. He had to smile when he saw she had reacted the same way.

"Still got those good reflexes," she said as they both sheathed their daggers. "Were you looking for me?"

A little off balance, Aahmes hesitated. "Uh…no?"

She chuckled. "You didn't drop off anything from last night. Bad night?"

"Oh, right. No, not bad. Just busy."

She leaned close and lowered her voice to a whisper. "I know Dar's got you hard at work on something. It's understandable you wouldn't be able to bring in your usual haul."

Aahmes glowered at her. "It's not a problem." He headed down the hallway toward the room next to Dar's. "We can take care of this now, if you'd like."

"Good thought," she muttered, with a hint of sarcasm, as she followed him.

She unlocked the door and waved him inside.

He pulled out his pouch and dumped it on the table,

holding back the few coins that belonged to him. Aerill counted the rest and gave him a sharp look.

"Reduced to pickpocketing again, are you?"

He shrugged, his expression bland and a bit bored. "Easy enough to still bring something back and not interfere with what I'm doing for our leader."

Aerill frowned but agreed with a sharp nod. "At least it will cover most of the bribe we need to get Macai back from the Warders. Again."

From the pile, she sorted out a navn—the gold coin of the Six Realms—and three vikls and pushed the coins toward him. "Your portion from last night…and the rest from the night before, which you seem to have forgotten to collect."

Aahmes studied her expression—seeing worry there—as he slipped the coins into his pouch. "It's that bad?"

Aerill gave him a shrewd look, followed by a quick nod. "If what you're working on is supposed to help, you might want to work faster," she whispered. "We're facing the risk of not meeting some of our regular bribes to various nobles, the way this is going."

Aahmes grimaced and glanced around the room. Even that casual look showed him that the Shadowers had brought much less to the Keep than usual for their nightly forays. "What's happening? Has anyone said?"

Aerill shrugged. "Various things, from what I've heard. Extra-vigilant Warders here, an opportunity lost there – all seemingly by chance, at first glance. But taken all together, none of it seems by chance. Some of our least experienced have been victims of pickpockets themselves. And even been attacked. Wounded." As she spoke, she walked to the chair behind the table and reached down to grab something from the floor.

Aahmes snorted at the idea of Shadowers allowing themselves to be pickpocketed, then almost choked in surprise when he saw what Aerill picked up from the floor: a wide strip of amber-colored cloth embroidered with rich, golden threads.

He must have made a sound because Aerill glanced at him, her expression questioning, the cloth hanging from her hand.

"Did one of them bring that?" Aahmes said as he tried to hide his reaction. "Why would someone steal such a thing?"

Aerill grinned and held it up, spreading it out between both hands to show Aahmes the whole thing. "This was brought in a while ago. That poor youngster believed the stitching was gold thread, but she was sadly mistaken. Turns out, it's not. So, while pretty, it's not worth much of anything. I decided to keep it for myself. I'd had it tucked away and just came across it again." She wrapped it around her shoulders and gestured toward the door.

"Shall we go. We're done here."

With a nod, Aahmes preceded her out the door, fighting despair. He had never expected the shawl to be in the hands of one of the guild's weapons instructors and the one person within the Shadowers with whom he knew he never wanted to seriously cross blades. It was widely said that no weapon existed that Aerill did not know how to use.

Aahmes watched her lock the door to the room and head down the hallway toward the stairs.

How was he going to get that cursed shawl?

CHAPTER 8

In the Keep's common hall, Aahmes nursed his drink and brooded about how to get the shawl. His friends at the table had offered dice to him, to join in their game, but he had declined.

He was not in the mood for a game of chance. He felt like he was already drowning in one.

Still almost two candle-marks away from the evening meal and the weapons-work Trial that would follow and Aahmes was uncertain what to do. After Dar himself, Aerill was perhaps the one person it would be most difficult to steal from. And now that she had been the one to show him the shawl, if it turned up missing from the Keep, he would be the first one she would come after.

Aahmes let his gaze roam around the room. Seemed that fewer people had gathered there than was usual for a late afternoon. Maybe they still roamed the city trying to get more loot. Maybe he should go find the rout again, demand some answers.

He noticed Namid was not in the room either. Hard at work on her Trial, no doubt.

With a sneer for that thought, he gulped the rest of his

drink and headed out to find a rout member. Maybe getting rid of some of his irritation would also let him come up with an idea for getting the shawl from Aerill that wouldn't come back on him in the future.

Aahmes sauntered through the areas of the city that used to be favored by the rout he had mixed with. He assumed that they haunted the same areas still, but after close to a candle-mark he had not spotted even one of the members he remembered. He frowned. Could they have moved to another area? Or might they have new members unknown to him so he would not spot them?

He headed to the underground hideout he had visited the previous night but found no one there. The tunnel that Clodarn and Phrae had exited through earlier only led to another room, fitted out with a place to cook and a few rough beds.

He wandered back upstairs and out into the waning afternoon. Without deciding to, his steps led him back toward Shadow Keep; there seemed nothing to accomplish out in the city right then.

Perhaps halfway back to the Keep, again following a tangled path, that sensation of being watched returned. A casual look around revealed no one obvious, but he knew they were there. One of them, at least.

He took himself in a direction away from the Keep and to less-frequented pathways, hoping to flush out his follower. Still, the other did not come out for another quarter candle-mark, although Aahmes had no trouble hearing the footsteps that trailed him. Aahmes was unsurprised to see that it was Gwelasius. While the big man's furtiveness had improved, he was still the noisiest of the rout members.

Gwel had chosen a small deserted alley to approach Aahmes, and he looked nervous, an unusual expression for him. Aahmes led the way off to the side, into a broken section of wall that offered an alcove difficult to see unless someone knew of it already.

It was crowded with the two of them there, but Gwelasius looked relieved to be out of sight.

"D'yeh have the shawl?" Gwel whispered.

"Are you supposed to collect it from me?" Aahmes countered.

"Aye. And if yeh didn't have it, I'm to give yeh a reason to work faster." Gwel clenched and unclenched his fists to make his meaning quite clear. Not that Aahmes needed clarification. The smash part of the rout's preferred smash-and-grab activities most often belonged to Gwel. But the big man did not look happy.

Aahmes peered at him, ready to draw his daggers if he needed to. But Gwel made no other move.

"So what's stopping you?" Aahmes said when it became clear Gwel was not going to attack him.

Gwel ducked his head and tucked his hands behind his back. "Aw, Aahmes, yeh always been decent enough to me, when yeh mixed with the rout. What they're plannin'…."

Aahmes leaned back against the other side of the alcove and crossed his arms. "What is it, Gwel? I *told* them today wasn't likely."

Gwel shuffled his feet and kept his gaze on them. "Not about that. Yeh know Berz don't like yeh…."

"Yeah."

"Well, him and Phrae been talkin' about what comes next. How they'll make sure yer Shadowers find out yeh stole from them. Make them think yeh been mixin' with the rout all along. How that'll help tear them apart."

"They really *are* going after the Shadowers, then."

Gwel nodded his head, his expression miserable. "Ain't good," he said. "We been doin' fine with what we do. Yer Shadowers do things different, their own way. It'll go bad. Fast, I'm thinkin'. I seen how good yeh've gotten and I know yeh'll not take this well. I'm not gonna be one gettin' killt in this."

"So you're planning to meet the deal so you can go

your own way?"

"Wish I could. Once even thought of maybe bein' a Warder. I'm strong enough. But the rout's not doin' the deal no more. I'm a good smasher, maybe the best, and they're keen on makin' sure I don't go."

He gave Aahmes a pleading look. "They can't find out I told yeh."

"They won't. You know I can keep secrets. What can you tell me of the person they have in the Shadowers? And would they really reveal where we hole up?"

Gwel barked a laugh, then looked alarmed at how loud he was. After he glanced around, he edged close.

"If they knew where yer hidey hole was, they'd have told already. And I don't know nothin' 'bout their sneak in with yer people. Maybe someone from one of the other routs this patron's got workin' for him."

"You're sure they don't know where we're at?"

Gwel nodded vigorously. "Dead sure. They're just foolin' yeh." He leaned to peer out of the alcove. "I gotta go. I'll say I ain't seen yeh yet. But even with what I said, yeh gotta get that shawl. Tomorrow, no later, like yeh said. What they been plannin' if yeh don't…it ain't good."

"What exactly *are* they planning?"

Gwel avoided his gaze. "I been too long. I gotta go," he mumbled and darted out of the alcove.

Aahmes took one step after him, then just let him go. After giving him enough time to get well away, Aahmes returned to his roundabout path toward the Keep, his thoughts occupied with what Gwel had told him. And what he hadn't.

He believed Gwel when he said that the rout did not know where the Keep was, but how had their sneak failed to tell them that? Some reason to keep it quiet from the rout? What could the sneak, and the rout, really be playing at?

And the rout meant to bring him down and the Shadowers with him, even though he'd agreed to get the cursed shawl? The more he pondered it, the more his anger grew.

Berz—and Phrae too, he knew—had never liked him. But trying to cross him earned them a lesson about why that was a bad idea. He'd find a way to turn that back on them.

~ ~ ~

That evening in the common hall, Aahmes tried to ignore the raucous goings-on around him. But his friends at the table insisted on speculating on the upcoming weapons-work portion of Namid's Trial. They rehashed every bit of sparring he and Namid had done in the past and argued over terms of the various wagers they wanted to make on him.

Still seething about the rout's plans, the little he knew, Aahmes picked at his food. Why had Gwel not wanted to tell him details? Was it that bad? Or was it a ruse to force him back with them? Or make him overthink the whole thing?

With a mental snarl at himself, he turned his attention to one problem he might actually be able to do something about. He took the opportunity to study the others gathered in the hall for the meal. Who could be the one who belonged to the rout?

The two learners Zwena and Orran were the newest. But Aahmes doubted it was either of them. They were too busy trying to learn to be Shadowers to have a chance to lurk and watch him and whatever else the rout might have their sneak doing.

He let his gaze roam around the room. He assumed it was someone relatively new to the Shadowers but, in truth, he had no solid reason to believe that it must be. No one struck him as even a remote possibility for the person he sought.

His gaze rested on Namid and he watched her fill her

plate a second time. An overfull stomach might work against her in the bout to come. *He* had not yet finished his first serving, a small one at that.

She caught him watching her. After a brief startled look, she gave him a wide grin before she turned away again.

Praiseworthy that she was able to act so confident. That would not last.

Aahmes was one of the last to finish his food. After the meal ended, and while he stacked his plate atop the rest off to the side for those assigned clean-up duty, other Shadowers moved the tables toward the sides of the large room.

Aahmes relished the sudden look of alarm that crossed Namid's face. Could she have forgotten about the weapons-work Trial? He grinned as he moved out of the way of those working to clear the center of the room.

CHAPTER 9

Through the crowd, Aahmes caught glimpses of Namid. She seemed to be looking for something. Him?

With a shrug, he moved to the far side of the room from her. Time to get ready for this.

While he worked through some warm-up moves he had learned as an apprentice, he caught glimpses again of Namid as she did the same. But his attention drifted away from the upcoming bout as he pondered what he would do when he next caught Berz. The anger that had begun to subside returned, with equal parts of frustration about the need to get that shawl.

He directed a glare Namid's direction. Jaikrein stood near her, giving her an encouraging talk it looked like.

At least he could take care of this problem with this bout. If she lost, or was too injured to complete the thievery portion, that would end the Trial.

When Jaikrein gestured to him, Namid paused in her own warm-up moves to glower at him.

Her Trial would also end if she backed out of any portion of it. Intimidation might work.

Aahmes drew two daggers and whirled through a series

of mock attacks at speed. He grinned as his actions rapidly cleared a space around him. He ended his attacks and gave Namid a cool gaze, interested to see what she would make of his display. Offering a silent challenge.

She seemed a little shaken. Good.

After a mocking bow for her, he turned away. Not all of a fight was one's skill with the weapons.

Aahmes glanced over his shoulder to see if it was having any effect on her. Seemed so, as it looked like Jaikrein might be reassuring her. Very good. This bout might already be half-won.

When Jaikrein pointed his direction, he turned his back again and found himself facing Aerill, who wore that cursed shawl. She gave him a narrow-eyed look, no doubt knowing exactly what he had been up to with his display. The slight smile she wore—which disappeared when she saw he had noticed it—proved she did. It was one of the things she taught apprentices, after all.

"About ready for this?" she said.

He answered with a grin.

With a curt nod for him, she gestured to include the two men who stood on either side of her. "We three will be the judges for the bout."

Aahmes inclined his head slightly to them all in greeting.

The man to Aerill's left, with weathered skin and graying hair and beard, was Thes. He was one of the oldest Shadowers, sometimes said to be of an age with Keizha, whatever age that was, and word had it he did 'special' tasks for Dar. He had been away much of the past few seasons working on something with Uffke—so the rumors said—the thin man with short black hair and skin darker than Aahmes' who stood to Aerill's right. Like Aerill, Uffke was a weapons instructor in the guild.

"You're a mite young, lad, t' be overseein' someone's Trial," Thes said.

"It's Namid's," Aerill said.

"Oh ho, this bout'll be one t' talk about, then."

"Thes!" Aerill's voice and expression were exasperated.

He shrugged, unrepentant. "Just sayin'."

"I might have to change my wager," Uffke muttered, his gaze on the far side of the room.

Aahmes turned in time to see Namid run through some quick mock attacks against the air as he had done. She was faster than he remembered. She must have worked on her weapons-work since they sparred last.

Even frustrated and angry, he still felt eager for this bout. He had always enjoyed the challenge she presented when they sparred.

Accompanied by the murmurs of wagers being made and the clink of coins changing hands, Dar stepped into the center of the room, a wooden box in his hands. He nodded to both Aahmes and Namid. After they stepped out to stand in front of him, he opened the box.

"You'll start with one of these, a matching one for each of you."

Aahmes considered the selection of knives in the box. The only real difference among them was the lengths of the blades.

He gave Namid a sidelong look as he grabbed one of the two with the shortest blades. With his longer reach, the dagger would give him a slight advantage. Would she take him up on his challenge? He held the knife out for her inspection and watched for her reaction.

When she became aware of his scrutiny, she shifted, as if uneasy. He grinned.

With a curt nod, she grabbed the matching knife.

Setting the box on the floor near the edge of the cleared area, Dar instructed them to leave their other blades with him.

Namid pulled out a couple of blades and handed them to Dar. Shortly, Dar also held all of Aahmes' various blades that he had carried hidden in a variety of spots about his person.

Aahmes rolled up the sleeves of his tunic to bare his forearms, a tradition in Shadower sparring to show that one had no hidden armor beneath the sleeves of shirt or tunic. Namid started to emulate him, then paused, catching Aahmes' attention.

Why had she stopped? With her sleeves rolled up partway, the armguards she wore most of the time were clearly visible, but that should not be a problem. They all knew of them and she only needed to remove them.

Aahmes studied her expression but could not guess what had stopped her. With an odd look on her face, she plopped down on the floor and worked at the laces of the armguards. Might it be something as simple as that she had forgotten how annoying it could be to have to unlace them?

Somehow, Aahmes had a feeling it was not anything that simple.

He backed up a couple of steps and watched as she seemed to make the whole thing more of a production than necessary. Maybe his little bit of intimidation had worked better than he had hoped. Might she be more reluctant to face him that she had been earlier because of it? Maybe she was trying to figure out a way out of it.

He almost laughed at that thought. *That* was not going to happen.

After she finally removed both armguards, she stood and handed them to Dar. Then she stepped back from the center as Aahmes had done, leaving a pace or so between them.

Could he have been wrong, and she really *was* working with Clodarn's rout? Aahmes peered at her, trying to see any sign of that.

She returned his look with a quizzical one of her own, her head tilted and a slight smile on her lips.

Was that a knowing smile?

With a nod for them both, Dar moved to the edge of the cleared area, still holding their personal weapons and now Namid's armguards, too.

Thes stepped forward and reviewed the few rules for the bout: they could use anything as a weapon, except their own blades that Dar held, and the bout would end at first blood or when the three judges called it.

After everyone retreated to line the walls, including the judges, Thes nodded to Aahmes and Namid. They slipped into knife-fighting stances and Aahmes attacked.

He managed to catch Namid in a grapple, although she briefly trapped his knife. She struggled to get free while still keeping him from slicing her, which would have ended the bout right then.

"You don't want to close with someone who's stronger than you," he murmured, his mouth right next to her ear. He shoved her hard, back away from him.

She kept to her feet somehow and glared at him.

Not giving her time to recover, he went for her again, right away. She scrambled away and satisfaction gripped him at the flash of fear he saw in her expression, gone the next instant. Still, his intimidation must be having some effect.

He kept after her, relentless and swift. One little scratch was all he needed, and one problem was gone from his life.

She retreated before his attacks, then managed to grab a second blade from the box of knives Dar had left for them.

Aahmes cursed to himself and tamped down his frustration. Letting her get that second knife had been a mistake. He needed to keep from making any others. Especially against this opponent. She had definitely improved since the last time they had sparred. This was not going to be as easy as he had expected.

With the second blade in hand, Namid went on the attack. She pursued him and kept him on the defensive. It was well done, but he needed to end this. The rout's threat weighed on him, demanding he be free to turn his attention there.

None of her attacks reached him. In the next instant, he regained the initiative, faster and more determined.

One slice from her blade almost reached his side. She was just too good now for him to be able to hold anything back and still win.

He answered her slice with a slash of his own, which she somehow dodged. She shook her head at him.

He laughed, denying her implied assertion that he would not win. It was only a matter of time and experience. He *would* get her.

They settled into a kind of dance, detached from the watchers, wills focused on their blades. Slice and stab.

And Namid blocked Aahmes' attempt to reach the box of knives.

A sudden clatter broke Aahmes' concentration. Had someone dropped some of the metal plates the Shadowers used at their meal? Could it have been intentional? That rout member, maybe.

Aahmes glanced that direction to see if he could spot the person who had made the noise. Namid lunged at him and he cursed himself for a fool – letting himself get distracted.

Entanglement and confusion left them both on the floor. They rolled away from each other as they raced to be first to stand again.

The end signal tore through the room, a shrill whistle that hurt Aahmes' ears as he had rolled close to the judges' feet.

Aahmes scrambled to his feet but stood where he was. Across the open space Namid did the same. The sight of the bleeding slash across Namid's forearm and her crumbling expression as she realized he had marked her with his blade brought a grin to his lips. The Shadowers began to mutter.

Sudden agony tore through Aahmes' arm and caused him to drop his knife. It hit the floor with a clang, and he clutched the bloody wound in his upper arm, pressing to try to slow the bleeding.

She had gotten him, too!

That miserable little tyro had managed to mark him at the same time.

He glowered at her, then glanced back at the judges. One by one, they all nodded, to Namid. So not only had she managed to fight him to a cursed draw, but she had also passed this portion of her Trial.

While the watching Shadowers surged forward after the judging, their Healer, Elnathan, fought his way to Aahmes. He was of an age with Aahmes, with skin and hair much like his as well. Elnathan set to work using his Healing Power on the wound.

Still new to Healing, he did little more than stop the bleeding. Then he bound the injury with a clean cloth and told Aahmes to try not to strain the wound too much, and maybe get some extra rest, if he could.

With a scowl for Namid, who sat on the floor and clutched her own wound, Aahmes walked over to Dar.

"A chance to talk?" he said as he retrieved his weapons from the older man.

"In my office. I'll be along soon."

Fuming at his injury, and the whole mess, Aahmes gave him a curt nod and headed to the stairs. He passed the three judges as they talked and laughed together on their way out a side door. Aahmes' gaze followed Aerill as an idea about how to get that shawl came to him.

CHAPTER 10

Waiting for the Shadowers' leader, Aahmes tried to lounge in one of the hard chairs in Dar's office. He mostly managed it, in spite of how unsuitable the chair was. He also tried to stay as still as possible, since any movement sent pains shooting through his arm. For each pang, he cursed that tyro under his breath.

He had cursed her half a dozen times before Dar joined him in the small room, closing the door behind him. With a questioning look for the younger man, he settled in one of the other chairs.

"You have something for me?"

Aahmes nodded and debated with himself about what he could tell Dar. Then a rush of anger cut that dissention short. He had no reason anymore to believe what the rout had told him, and he did not owe them anything anyway.

But first things first. *Someone might hear,* he told Dar, using hand-talk, the silent language of the Shadowers that they all learned after they passed their Trials. Aahmes wished he could tell Dar everything with hand-talk, but he was still learning it.

Understood, Dar replied the same way.

"I feel a need to be out this night. Walk with me," Dar said aloud as he stood again and headed out the door.

With an almost-stifled groan, Aahmes followed.

"She got you pretty good," Dar said.

Aahmes glowered at him and Dar chuckled.

"You got her nearly as good," Dar added. "Her wound might affect her thievery, so I'll consider the injury another of those extra challenges for her Trial. And that's the end of any additional challenges. Let her Trial run now as it will."

Aahmes nodded and followed Dar down the stairs and out of the Keep through a small side door, avoiding the still-crowded common hall. Staying hidden, they followed several random streets away from the Keep to a large open square nearby, never busy at the best of times and deserted that time of day.

Dar sat on the edge of the well at the square's center and motioned Aahmes to join him there. With a quick look into the well to make certain no one lurked there, Aahmes perched on the low wall.

"Tell me," Dar said.

So Aahmes told him, his voice not much louder than a whisper. He told Dar about the 'patron' who was uniting rascals and the rout's claim that they had someone within the Shadowers watching, ready to tear them down if Aahmes did not do as he was supposed to, and the new information that they were probably going to try it anyway.

Dar frowned when Aahmes finished.

"What is it you're supposed to do?" he said.

"Steal from the Shadowers," Aahmes said.

Dar's frown deepened and he nodded. "That would certainly tear at us, create a rift that someone could use."

"But if I don't bring them the item, they sound like they have other plans, too."

Dar nodded. "What's the item they want?"

Aahmes gave Dar a long look. "I'd rather not say. I have an idea how to get it that won't be traced back to me or anyone in the Shadowers. But if something goes wrong, you can't be linked to it in any way."

Dar pondered that at some length before he agreed.

"There *is* something you can help me with," Aahmes said. "It's why I wanted to talk. Can you get me a meeting with one of the other nearby rout leaders? I've got a couple of questions that I don't trust my old rout with – and maybe an idea."

Dar stood with a nod. "I'll arrange it. You heading out into the city?"

Aahmes grinned. "Of course. It's full dark soon, it's time for us to be out and about."

"Of course. You might want to change out of the bloodied clothes before you go." Dar matched Aahmes' grin and headed away from the square. *Not* back to Shadow Keep, Aahmes noticed.

Aahmes glanced at his torn and bloody sleeve, with the bandage wrapped around his arm clearly visible through the rent in the cloth. Dar made a good point.

~ ~ ~

Aahmes ended up changing all of his clothes. He hauled out his most ragged tunics and trousers to mimic the way most rout members looked. He carried several knives, but none openly like he usually did. And he quietly cursed Namid as he worked around the pain from his wound to change clothes. With a cap settled low on his head, he was set.

He slipped out of the Keep, making certain no one saw him, and headed toward the closest taverns. If he had guessed right, he ought to find Aerill, Thes and Uffke having a few drinks to welcome back the two who had been absent from the Keep for so long.

Aahmes reasoned that if Aerill's shawl disappeared while she was out in the city, it was far less likely that anyone, especially within the guild, would link the theft to a Shadower, and to him in particular. A busy tavern should give him some kind of opportunity to filch the thing.

That was his plan anyway.

The first four taverns Aahmes checked were busy, as expected, but no Aerill. He also watched for any rout members but spotted no one who looked like rout.

At the fifth tavern, smaller and more crowded than the previous ones, Aahmes finally spotted Aerill. She sat at a small table in a back corner with Thes and Uffke. From the look of it, they were having a good time. She still wore the shawl.

Aahmes slipped back outside to a hidden spot from which to watch the door while he considered his next move. He needed a distraction. And how was he to get her to take off the shawl? It had been warm in the tavern and yet she still wore it. He preferred not to get close enough to grab it from her shoulders, even assuming he could.

He watched the tavern as he pondered his options. A brawl would be the easiest distraction, although not at all original. But such a thing worked...plenty of noise and confusion.

He brushed stray strands of his hair back from his face and winced at the pain in his arm. This was likely to give him even more injuries. Still….

With a sigh, he returned to the tavern and eased inside, keeping to the other side of the crowded room from the Shadowers' table. He scanned the tavern patrons as he pushed his way through them, looking for the likeliest to begin the trouble.

This could be fun!

He ignored the muttered protests in his wake—they would only add to the confusion—and located a couple of men who looked well into their cups. They stood almost back to back as they laughed with their own circles of friends.

He increased his pace and poked one of them in the shoulder and bumped the other as he slipped past, then watched as they drunkenly demanded explanations of each other. When both tried to deny doing anything, it escalated from there. He slipped to a place along one wall and kept Aerill in sight as the altercation spread throughout the room.

Aahmes headed for the three Shadowers when they stood, looking like they planned to leave. He again shoved his way through the crowd and added jabs with his elbows as needed for his purposes, dodging any blows aimed at him.

When only one man stood between him and Aerill, he shoved him hard, to knock him into her back. Then he ducked down and scrambled around the direction Aerill did not turn, clutching the man's arm to guide his hand so it caught her shawl as he tried to regain his lost balance.

Aahmes stumbled a couple of steps as the man almost took him down with him. He fell against a table, then ducked when Aerill looked around. When she turned away again, Aahmes grabbed a fallen mug and tossed it hard on a nearby woman's feet to draw her attention to the Shadowers. When the woman charged at them, he snagged the shawl from the floor, stuffed it under his tunic, and scuttled away under the tables to the door.

He managed to get outside suffering from only a few bruises and one unfortunately accurate punch that had connected with his wounded arm.

Two steps into the night a hard grip on his arm—right on his wound—halted him and spun him around. The pain almost dropped him to his knees.

"My shawl," Aerill growled in his face.

Aahmes winced, and not just from the pain. A quick look around showed him that at least Thes and Uffke were not with her.

With a desperate glance at her irate expression, he tried to think of something to tell her.

She glared at him and gave his arm a hard shake, which sent agony slicing through it. "Don't bother trying to come up with a good story," she warned.

He nodded and tilted his head toward the side of the building. "Not out here, please?"

With a curt nod, she hauled him where he indicated and around the corner, out of sight of anyone within the still-riotous tavern.

"Talk."

Aahmes shrank under her hard gaze. "I don't know what I should tell you. It's part of this thing Dar has me working on."

Her expression turned incredulous. "*Dar* had you steal my shawl?"

"No! He doesn't even know about this. But I need it as part of what I'm doing for him. For us, the Shadowers."

Aerill frowned at him. "My shawl?" she repeated.

Aahmes nodded, his expression miserable. But he sighed in relief when she released his arm.

She folded her arms and scowled at him. "You couldn't have asked for it?"

He shook his head.

She sighed and looked him up and down. "Looks like it must've been taken by one of those rout vermin," she said with a hint of a smile. "I'm sure I saw one scuttle off from the tavern."

Aahmes dared to give her a hopeful look. "I'd say that's a fair description," he ventured.

She snorted. "Fine. But you now owe me." She leaned into his face. "And I will collect what you owe. In full."

Then she stomped off.

Aahmes resettled his cap, which had been knocked askew, and took himself into the darkness of the city's alleys to stash the shawl in a safe hiding place until he took it to the rout.

CHAPTER 11

Aahmes returned to Shadow Keep as unseen as when he left it. After he shed his rags and hid them away, he flopped across his bed and drifted into welcome sleep…until someone shook him awake.

It seemed that little time had passed, but he at least felt somewhat rested. Perhaps it had been longer than it seemed. He blearily focused his eyes, then sat up abruptly.

"Dar?"

Dar put a finger across his lips.

Meet outside The Frowning Shoe tavern, he told Aahmes using hand-talk. He kept to signs Aahmes would know well, although he had to spell out the name of the tavern so the younger man would understand. *Show this.*

Dar handed him a small stone on a black cord, while aloud he said he was just checking on Aahmes and his wound. The stone was gray and shaped like a raindrop.

Go now, Dar told him and left the room.

Aahmes scrambled to his feet. He pulled a couple of tunics over his shirt and trousers, grabbed several knives to secret about himself, and snatched his cloak. His roommate was not in his bed so Aahmes assumed it was still sometime before dawn. The other man seldom returned to the Keep until then, and it was not unusual for the two of them to not encounter each other for days at a time.

Aahmes used all his skills to creep through the building. He made it outside without encountering anyone. He took to the back alleys and some shortcuts he knew and hurried to The Frowning Shoe tavern, which sat near the West Gate of the city.

Close to a candle-mark after he left the Keep, Aahmes approached the tavern. He saw no one outside and few people inside through the open door.

He stayed in the shadows to circle around to the back and spotted someone lingering there, also in the shadows. He held up the token Dar had given him and stepped into the dim light from the lamp at the end of the alley.

The other person turned toward him, then approached. When the figure got closer, Aahmes saw it was a boy, with light brown skin and hair, some winters younger than himself, he judged. The boy looked him over.

"Who sent yeh?" he whispered.

"Dar," Aahmes whispered back.

The boy nodded and walked past him, headed to another alley.

"Come on with yeh, then. This way," he tossed back over a shoulder.

The boy led Aahmes several streets away to a rundown building that looked like a house. They entered and climbed the stairs to the second floor. The boy indicated a door to the side of the landing before he returned back down the stairs.

After a look down the hallway in the gloom, and seeing no one, Aahmes tapped on the door.

A man perhaps a few winters older than Aahmes opened the door. His hair was almost as dark as Aahmes' own, while his skin was much lighter. He had a short beard and mustache and stood perhaps a handspan shorter than

Aahmes. He beckoned him inside.

After the man closed the door behind them, someone unshuttered a lantern just enough to allow Aahmes to somewhat see the other two occupants of the room, both women. One held herself like a guard and fingered the long daggers at her hips. She also had dark hair and light skin, similar to the man's but not so much as to make Aahmes think they might be related.

But it was the other woman who grabbed Aahmes' attention. She wore a simple, ankle-length dress with a heavy cloak of some pale color. Hard to tell what color in the dim light. Her hair and skin both looked white. Her eyes were a little darker, but not by much. She looked no older than himself.

She smiled at him. "I'm Liakae. I lead our rout with my brother Ikyas." She gestured at the man, who now leaned against the wall off to one side. Then she reached out to the woman and clasped hands with her. "And here's my companion Reka, who keeps us both safe."

Aahmes gave a nod of greeting and introduced himself.

Liakae's smile widened. "We know who you are. The only former rout member to earn a place with the Shadowers. Best thief among the routs." She settled herself in a chair and waved a hand at the shuttered lantern. "You must find this rather dramatic. It's not intended so. Well, except maybe for the dress. I wanted to look nice for a visit from one of the esteemed Shadowers. The rest is because too much light hurts my eyes."

Uncertain how to respond, Aahmes just smiled slightly. "I thank you for agreeing to meet with me. I hope you might answer a couple of questions for me?"

Liakae and Ikyas exchanged glances. "Let's hear them," Ikyas said.

"First, have you heard of someone who's trying to gather together all the routs? Make them one, perhaps? Has that person approached you?"

"Yes, to all," Liakae said with a laugh, a delighted

sound that made Aahmes smile with her. "And I anticipate your next question…. No, we want nothing to do with it."

That was good. One possible complication easily taken care of. "Then you know who this person is? Clodarn mentioned a patron—"

The rout members' laugher cut off what he was saying. When they sobered somewhat, Ikyas explained.

"We do know who it is. And there's no 'patron' involved. It's Clodarn who's trying to do this. He thinks much of himself and would have all the rest of us bow to him like he's some noble."

Aahmes nodded. "In that case, I'd wager my next question will appeal to you. Would you be interested in helping me ruin Clodarn's rout? I'd just ask for a kindness for one of the members."

Liakae rose to her feet with a grace that would not have been out of place in a noble's house. She glided close to Aahmes and placed a light hand on his shoulder, gazing at him from little more than a handspan away. Her eyes were nearly on a level with his own and he now saw that they were a unique pale purple.

"Intriguing. I can see advantages and opportunities in such a partnership…." She leaned closer and Aahmes found himself drawn into her unusual eyes.

After a breath-of-time, he shook himself as he remembered Feona's smile. He brushed his hair from his face and took a slight step back. "I don't doubt it. But only something limited."

She smiled and twirled away from him in a billow of her skirt. "Ah, ease into it. Nice."

Ikyas cleared his throat. "What are you asking us to do?"

"Simply see that the Warders hear that Clodarn and his rout have something that belongs to one of the nobles. Something that was stolen from her. Something she'd like back, I'm sure. They don't have it yet, but I'll let you know when they do. Then you get word to the Warders."

"Simple enough," Ikyas said. He exchanged glances again with his sister, then they both nodded. "We're in."

"And what of this kindness for one of them?" Reka spoke for the first time.

"One of them is not involved in the schemes. He just does what they say. For the most part."

Again the brother and sister exchanged looks.

"Gwel, right?" Reka said.

Aahmes nodded.

"We're friendly," Reka said. "I think I can convince him."

"We've wanted to get Gwel to mix with our rout," Liakae said at the same time.

"Then we agree," Ikyas said to Aahmes. "When?"

"No later than a day from now. Can I send a messenger to one of you? When it's set."

"The boy who met you near The Frowning Shoe. He can wait there for your messenger."

Aahmes agreed with a curt nod. "The messenger will bring him this token of yours." He held up the stone on its cord. "And she'll tell him 'It's time'. Then the Warders will just need to get to the rout's hideaway.

"The one that's a street north of the old Bigge Smithy?" Liakae said.

Aahmes nodded. "Is that good enough?"

The rout members nodded their agreement.

As Aahmes started through the door to leave, Liakae called after him, "And do come back again to visit. We can explore more partnering ideas."

On his way back to the Keep, something Liakae had said came back to him.

"'Only former rout member to earn a place among the Shadowers'..." he muttered. That had to mean there were no other rout members in the guild. And that had to mean Clodarn had lied about them having someone in the Shadowers.

Aahmes grinned. With the shawl taken care of and now

this visit, it had been a good night.

~ ~ ~

Dawn had begun to color the sky when Aahmes returned to the Keep. A quick peek into Namid's room showed him that she had not yet returned. She would probably be back soon, then.

He leaned against the doorframe of a vacant room down the hall from hers to wait, to see her when she returned. After all, he *should* check on her Trial progress.

Not a quarter candle-mark later, she returned, stumbling into the hall. She looked haggard, weary. With a grimace, she stopped when she saw him.

He grinned. "Late night, last night?"

"Now, where would you get that idea?" she snarled back.

He held his smile and shrugged. "I hope your wound isn't paining you too much."

"I hope yours *is*!"

Aahmes grinned even more as he reminded her that time was running short.

"I'm not likely to forget how much time is left!" She pulled two navns from a pouch and tossed them to him. "Here. Now shut up and leave me alone."

She pushed past him, headed for her room.

Aahmes tucked the navns away with a laugh. Two navns richer – this had indeed been a good night!

CHAPTER 12

Aahmes slept later than usual the next morning, until around midday, and felt better for it. He rushed through a scrabbled-together meal and headed out into the city. Time to squelch this rout trouble.

He looked forward to it.

For his first task, he needed to find that messenger girl. He carried all his coins with him this day and expected his pouch to be much lighter by the end of all this. But it would be worth it.

After close to two candle-marks of looking and asking about her, Aahmes finally located her. Her practiced smile of greeting turned genuine when he approached.

The girl was more than happy to run more messages for him, and even give him the whole day, for the coins he handed her. He learned that the coins would let her start an apprenticeship she had been saving for. And he learned her name was Aza.

"Vayaza, really" she told him, wrinkling her nose in displeasure. "Some sorta minstrel Ma really likes. She wanted to be like her, but Ma don't sing near as good." Aza chuckled a little at that, then told Aahmes where to find her more readily the next time, should he want to have her run errands again.

He gave her two errands to start: two messages to deliver in the order he detailed. First, she needed to find the big man in Clodarn's rout that she had spoken with before—something she assured him would be no problem—and tell him to stay away from the rout, and better yet, to visit The Frowning Shoe tavern for several good long drinks.

For her second task, he asked her to deliver a message to someone else in Clodarn's rout, saying that Aahmes would have what they wanted at midnight, in the hidden place. He told Aza to deliver the message and *not* wait for an answer, to just keep out of sight until he needed her for the next task that night.

With those arrangements made, Aahmes set out across the city to the place he had hidden the shawl.

As he made his way through back alleys and shortcuts, he wondered what Namid was doing. She had this day and night left to get the statue. Was she going to make it?

From the way she had looked at dawn, Aahmes would not be surprised if she still slept. He hoped she did, in fact. If her time ran short, she ought to feel harried and be more prone to make mistakes.

With some lurking about followed by a little lock-picking, Aahmes retrieved the shawl from where he had hidden it in the cellar of Feona's tavern. Then out again, locking the door behind him.

Heading back across the city, taking his time, he noticed the light beginning to fade. He decided to wait until after dark for the next part of his plan. It would probably be easier then, anyway, as the rout would have moved out into the city for their usual nighttime smash-and-grab activities.

Might as well stop off at the Keep and get something to eat. Although by the time he got there, the evening meal might be over. But there should still be some food he could snatch.

On the way, he settled the shawl more securely. He placed it at his back between his inner tunic and his shirt, with his belt helping hold it, and his cloak over all to help hide it.

He heard a couple of raised voices further down the street, men shouting lewd offers to someone. He recognized Namid as the focus of their interest. When one of them persisted in bothering her and she silenced him with the threat of her stiletto at his throat before she walked off, Aahmes laughed without a sound.

Looked like she was headed for the Keep, like he was. He hurried to get there first and waited for her at the door.

"Got the Star yet?" he said and greeted her with a toothy grin at the same time.

After a startled glance, she made a show of checking all her pouches. "Seems not," she said and gave him one of those overly sweet smiles. "Patience, oh anxious Trial overseer. I still have time."

"Time that is growing shorter and shorter."

"Oh? You've noticed that too, huh?"

He glared at her. Irritating to have his taunting manner thrown back at him.

"You won't be so cheerful at dawn," he said after a breath-of-time.

"I won't?" she said, with a blatantly innocent look. "Perhaps."

She brushed past him and walked away. "We shall see, won't we?"

Aahmes lingered there until he saw her carry some food from the kitchen toward her room. Then he stepped inside to grab something for himself.

He devoured his meal then headed back to the hideaway that the rout had showed him. He used all his skills with stealth to pass unnoticed, and kept alert for anyone who might be looking for him.

He saw Phrae on his way back, but she was involved in

intimidating a young noble who had ventured too far into the wrong ring of the city. As he passed them, Aahmes also spotted Berz lurking nearby, waiting to step in if Phrae needed it. Neither of them saw him.

He did not see Gwel. He hoped that meant he had taken himself away from Clodarn's rout.

Aahmes took the time to check all around the hideaway. No sign of any of the rout, so he slipped inside, making his way by feel in the dark to tuck the shawl under the bedding of one of the beds in the back room. He made certain to put the bedding back as it had been before, then hurried back out and away.

Aahmes then headed back to find Aza in the place she had told him to look for her.

Handing over another coin, he asked her to deliver one last message: the one to Ikyas and Liakae's rout. Then he told her to find a place to hide for a couple of days. Aza promised that she would and ran off.

Aahmes headed back to Clodarn's rout's hideaway, taking even more care, if possible, to pass unnoticed.

He found a perch on the roof of a nearby building that was less run-down than most in that area and settled in to wait. He did not want to miss this.

His wait extended long enough that he dozed some. But the scrape of a boot on the stones of the street woke him. A single street-lantern provided dim light for the area. Aahmes watched three Warders enter the hideaway, while others remained outside on guard. He counted eight of them, including the ones inside.

When the three returned outside, all the Warders conferred in a huddled group before they settled themselves around the hideaway in places that hid them from anyone who might approach. Because of where he lurked, Aahmes could see most of them.

Less than a quarter candle-mark later, footsteps heralded the approach of the rout. Aahmes watched Berz, Phrae and Clodarn enter the hideaway, followed by four others he did not know. The Warders followed them inside, almost stepping on their heels.

The sounds of a scuffle and some shouts came from the hideaway and soon thereafter the rout members were marched back out, hands secured behind them. They looked a little worse for their encounter. One of the Warders carried the shawl, and also a small bag that clinked as it swung in her hand.

Aahmes cursed to himself at missing out on that little bit of loot. He should have thought to poke around in there when he left the shawl.

Keeping close watch on their prisoners, the Warders hustled the rout members away.

Aahmes waited until long after they left before he budged from his hiding spot. Even then, he took extra care to stay unseen. He would not be surprised if the Warders had someone still watching the hideaway with plans to capture anyone else who came there.

When he was well away, he broke into a wide grin and danced a few steps from a festive dance he remembered from his childhood. With all of his other problems with this rout thing, that part had gone well.

He sobered as he headed back to the Keep, following a convoluted route to throw off any possible followers. He needed to be at the Keep when that tyro staggered back defeated. Yet another thing he did not want to miss. He even managed to snatch a couple of hefty coin pouches on his way.

~ ~ ~

Aahmes waited perhaps a candle-mark before he saw Namid approaching the Keep. She was early. He estimated the night still had about a candle-mark left. While he had waited, he had noticed many other Shadowers taking positions nearby. He was not the only one eager to see the end of this Trial.

He stepped out from the shadows near the Keep's main entrance and approached her. The others edged closer also.

"Well?" he said, when Namid stepped close.

She handed him a sack. Aahmes loosened its top and peered inside.

It couldn't be – but it was!

He glanced at her in amazement. Somehow, she had managed it. Impressive!

Aahmes pulled out the statue and held it high for all to see.

The sudden press of Shadowers who jostled to congratulate Namid pushed him aside and carried her through the door into Shadow Keep.

Before the crowd carried her out of sight, Namid called back to him, "Your turn!"

CHAPTER 13

After the last of the jubilant Shadowers streamed into the Keep, Aahmes ambled along the street to a secluded alcove. He tucked himself within and crouched down to consider the statue in his hands.

He truly had not expected her to be able to snatch it, this slip of a girl. So, he had not given any thought to how he would return the thing before the mage came looking for it. But now he had to, and soon. He had half a day after its theft to get it back to the mage. Another trouble, now his.

He did not want to learn what would happen if he missed that deadline. Just in case the tale was true.

Aahmes pondered how to return the statue while he turned it around in his hands and admired the valuable jewel set into the center of the distorted star shape. If he could pry that out....

He tried to work a fingernail under the edge of the setting. But no luck.

He considered the possibilities. Namid had returned before dawn, and she had not been winded as if she had hurried back to the Keep. So she probably took the statue from the mage's stronghold at least two candle-marks before she had handed it over. That would have been time enough to cross the city in no hurry. Or maybe she hurried then rested before she came the rest of the way to the Keep.

Of course, she could have grabbed it before that, which would mean he had less time. But as long as he got the thing back to its owner no later than about midday, he judged, he should be fine. Or just got it away from Shadow Keep and out of any Shadower's hands.

Could he somehow wrangle something for himself from this? Maybe get the mage to give him some reward for the statue's return? After a little thought he shook his head. Too impractical. Not to mention riskier than the reward would be worth. He did not want to catch the mage's attention.

If it were still night, he could sneak back out to the stronghold and slip the statue through the gate. But it was already growing too bright for such a move. He needed another idea.

Aahmes felt a peculiar tingle in his fingertips. Could the mage's Power already be doing something to locate the statue? He tucked the Star back into its bag and secured it to the back of his belt, under his cloak. Time to figure out what to do with it, how to get it back to the mage.

He headed to the city ring where most of the caravanners stayed. He remembered Namid had visited there a couple of days earlier. To set up something that had helped her in the Trial, he suspected. Maybe he would find some inspiration there himself.

He kept to the back alleys and hidden ways as much as possible, as usual. He did not even have to think about it. Instead his thoughts wandered to Namid.

Roughly two winters earlier, she had shown up at the Keep out of nowhere, at Dar's heels. She could not have seen more than about sixteen winters then, which made her a couple of winters younger than Aahmes, more or less. And yet she had soon challenged Aahmes' position as the best newcomer to the guild.

Moreover, something about her caught his attention, and not just that she looked like she could be his sister. Although he had soon realized they only looked so much alike when her features were still. When she smiled or laughed, even when she glared at him, she did not look so much like him at all.

At first, he had watched her to try to figure out the trick...why she had come to the Shadowers. But soon after, he had found that he looked for her, hoped to catch sight of her wherever the Shadowers gathered. She drew him somehow, the unaffected grace in her movements, even when they sparred, the spark in her gaze when they bantered.

But it was a horrible idea to let himself notice such things.

So, while she served her apprenticeship and worked to learn the skills she would need, he had worked to create and keep a distance, a barrier formed of scorn and dislike between them. That way no one who knew anything about him would have any reason to think that she was anything to him.

Because she wasn't.

And now she had completed her Trial. That made her a full Shadower...and made her presence that much harder for him.

What if they were teamed? Would Dar do that? Send them out together? With their skills, they could make a formidable team.... Aahmes scowled at his thoughts and forced the imagined possibilities away.

Stay away from her and concentrate on the task at hand, *tyro*, he berated himself as he brushed his hair back out of his eyes. Letting your mind wander.... Just return the cursed statue to that cursed mage. *There* is where to focus your attention.

When he reached the ring that held the lodgings the

caravanners favored, he lurked about the edges of the inn yards. He helped at several with loading and unloading wagons and cursed from time to time at the pain in his arm from where *that girl* had sliced him. He picked up a few coins and a lot of gossip and moved on to the next inn. Nothing yet about anything missing from the mage's hold.

Good news, he decided.

Late in the morning, Aahmes found his solution. A caravan that had just arrived hired him, and several others, to unload part of one wagon so the traders could send it on to the mage's hold with the rest of the cargo.

After the hired workers unloaded a little more than half the wagon—all sacks of something—several barrels still sat in the wagon. When the others moved on to other jobs, Aahmes investigated. They all seemed to be wine barrels.

He smiled. This would be unique.

He found one barrel that had an ill-fitted lid and managed to pry it open. His injury pulled painfully with the effort. A glance at his arm showed blood seeping through the wrappings and the shirt he wore. He cursed in a quiet voice.

Aahmes slipped the Star out of its bag and eased it into the wine. After he settled it on the bottom of the barrel, he closed the barrel again. With a quick look around to make sure no one paid him any special attention, he pounded on the lid to get it sealed again the best he could. Then he watched for the traders to return.

And the time slipped away.

They must be enjoying a rest along with a good meal inside.

Aahmes fidgeted. That statue had to get back to the mage's hold!

As midday drew too near, he ventured inside the inn and found the man who had hired him to help unload the goods that were not going to the mage.

He took on the demeanor of a man desperate for coin

and approached the man with diffidence.

"Beggin' yer pardon f'r interruptin' good sir," he said when the man glanced at him. "If p'rhaps yeh'd rather enjoy yer time here longer, I c'n take th' wagon across to th' mage's hold. I c'n use more coin. Got m' old aunt to take care of."

The man studied him and took a long pull on his drink.

"Save you a trip," one of his companions urged. "And I saw this fellow workin' hard out there earlier."

"How'd I know you won't run off with the wagon and cargo?" the man demanded of Aahmes.

Aahmes cringed beneath his accusation. "N-never. I wouldna even think o' trying to make off wi' something o' the mage's. Don't want to be turned into a mouse. Or somethin' worse!"

The traders all laughed and the man Aahmes had approached clapped him on the shoulder, his injured one, unfortunately. Aahmes fought to keep from showing how much that hurt.

"Smart man," the trader said and handed him two vikls. "Run the load across and there's a navn for you when you bring the wagon and horses back here."

Aahmes ducked his head and bowed. "Thank yeh, thank yeh. I'll take it over now."

He all but ran to the wagon, then drove it as fast as he dared through the streets to the East Gate, the passing time and his awareness of the statue behind him urging speed. That peculiar tingle prickled across his back now.

When he told the guard at the gate his destination, the man waved him through without any further delay.

The faintest of trails from previous wagons marked the short distance to the mage's hold, and Aahmes had a rough ride, going as fast as he was. A few paces shy of the gate, Aahmes noticed a low hum coming from behind him.

Before he could react, the hum became a sudden roar. Something shook the ground and threw him from the wagon. He landed hard, although he managed to roll to take some of the hurt out of it, thanks to lessons from the weapons-trainers.

His vision dimmed from the pain from his wound and he fought to stay conscious.

Rolling over, he looked back toward the wagon, or rather where the wagon had been. He had been flung fully five paces, perhaps more.

He stared as he tried to understand what he saw.

The wagon was gone. Obliterated. In its place a pillar of what looked like silver fire rose to the sky. Aahmes watched the wagon's horses race away. At least they had escaped harm. Behind the fiery pillar, he glimpsed some people in the mage's courtyard picking themselves up from the ground.

The upper part of the silvery fire swayed back and forth and the whole thing shaped itself into a paces-high duplicate of the Star. It held the shape for several long breaths-of-time.

Then the flames shrank back to the ground and vanished, revealing the statue itself sitting upright where the wagon had been. The breeze from that direction brought an acrid-burnt odor that wafted past Aahmes and made his eyes burn.

Someone in robes crossed the mage's courtyard and approached the statue.

Aahmes yanked the hood of his cloak over his head, scrambled to his feet and ran for the gates of Rhadanthus. He saw a crowd at the city gates retreat inside at the same time – no one wanted to encounter the mage or attract his attention.

Aahmes plunged through the gate into the midst of what was left of the crowd, avoiding the questions of the gate guard. He stayed with the crowd at first and let it take him further back into the city. When he decided that it was time to be elsewhere, he slipped away.

He paused in a shaded alley and leaned against the wall until he stopped shaking.

That had been too close!

But now he knew how the mage could find his statue.

He grinned. No Shadower would doubt that he had returned the statue. His reputation was intact, maybe even enhanced after that spectacle. Soon the city would be filled with fantastic tales of what had happened at the mage's hold.

As Aahmes sauntered along the street, headed toward Shadow Keep, his home, he frowned to himself. Now how to avoid that girl....

~

Notes and Pronunciations

A week is eight days long.

A "candle-mark" is roughly equivalent to an hour.

A "breath-of-time" is an indeterminate short amount of time, roughly seconds to a few minutes.

A "pace" is the length of a double step (roughly five feet).

Aahmes -- AH mehz
Aahms -- AHMZ
Aerill -- AY rihl
Aza -- AY zuh

Berz -- BUHRZ
Bigge -- BIHG

Carssi -- KAHR see
Chendrukhar -- CHEHN droo kahr
Clodarn -- CLOH dahrn
Corentris -- kohr EHN trihss

Dar -- DAHR

Elnathan -- EL nuh thuhn
Ezeor -- EH zee ohr

Feona -- fee OH nuh

Gwel -- GWEL
Gwelasius -- gwel AZ yuhss

Hadelin -- HAH duh lihn

Ikyas -- IHK yuhss

Jai -- JAY
Jaikrein -- JAY kr-eye-n

Keizha -- K-EYE zhuh
korz -- KOHRZ

Liakae -- LEE uh kay

Macai -- MAH kay

Namid -- NAH meed
navn -- NAH vuhn

Orran -- OH ruhn

Phrae -- FRAY

Reka -- REE kuh
Rhadanthus -- ruh DAN thuhss

Thes -- THEHSS

Uffke -- OOV keh

Vayaza -- vuh YAY zuh
vikl -- VIH kuhl

Walrard -- WAHL ruhrd

Zwena -- ZWEHN uh

~

Titles by S. Lynn Helton

Wild Heritance fantasy series

Duplicity of Power
Power Awry
Power Redeemed

Trial Run (prequel novella)
Trial and Tribulation (prequel novella)

The Deliberia Chronicles fantasy trilogy

Crystalborne Sigils
Songborne Gates
A Galeborne Resolve

Author's Note

Thank you for reading my book. I hope you enjoyed it!

Please consider leaving an honest review on the book's
product page at your favorite online bookstore
and on Goodreads. Reviews from readers like you are
powerful and greatly help other readers
discover books they might enjoy.

-Lynn

About the Author

S. Lynn Helton lives in the foothills of the Rocky
Mountains, U.S.A., with her family and a couple of crazy
cats. Lynn enjoys camping and hiking, playing games,
crafting, reading (a lot) and, of course, writing.

Read more about her books on her website:
www.slynnhelton.com